Secret of Jewel Creek

Marshal Seth Benteen's problems start when he comes across a wagon in a creek with a busted wheel which is carrying a secret cargo of gold. Jewel Creek has fallen on hard times and were word to get out trouble would soon follow. But for whom was the smuggled gold destined?

Could it be the Freedom Brotherhood, a secret organization rumoured to be preparing for a revolution? Benteen hides the gold in the town jail but as the night wears on it is stolen and a friend he had confided in is murdered.

Benteen must recover the gold and solve the murder if he is to stop a revolution and save his own life.

By the same author

Kirk's Law
Ruben's Ruse
Robb's Stand
Hangman's Lot
Flint's Bounty
Fast Gun Range
Rope Justice
Ponderfoot's Dollars

Secret of Jewel Creek

Ben Coady

A Black Horse Western

ROBERT HALE · LONDON

ISBN-10: 0-7090-8122-7
ISBN-13: 978-0-7090-8122-7

Robert Hale Limited
Clerkenwell House
Clerkenwell Green
London EC1R 0HT

Typeset by
Derek Doyle & Associates, Shaw Heath
Printed and bound in Great Britain by
Antony Rowe Limited, Wiltshire

CHAPTER ONE

Marshal Seth Benteen checked the time by the law office clock – midnight. Twelve hours he would have to wait for the noon train to arrive, if it arrived on time – if it arrived at all. If the storm that was blowing did not wash out the track or a bridge. If the Creighton gang, led by Benny Creighton, a cut-throat without a smidgen of conscience, who had busted out of the State Penetentiary, did not arrive in town before the train to settle old scores as he promised he would two years previously. If the brooding mood of Jewel Creek – the kind of mood that grips a down-on-its-knees town – did not explode. A lot of ifs when there was a quarter of a million dollars in gold from an unknown source and therefore easily stolen, stashed in the jail behind the marshal's office.

Bentcen pondered glumly on any one of a

hundred things that could go wrong, while listening for every creak and sigh of the wind to try and figure out what kind of trouble might be coming his way. No one knew that stashed in a cell in the jailhouse was the kind of treasure that would collectively lift Jewel Creek out of its slide into poverty or, alternatively, make one or a couple of men very rich men indeed. The treasure was disguised, hidden inside a plain wooden crate marked: Farm Implements. And he was the only man in Jewel Creek who knew what the box really contained. Which left him exclusively with a mountain of worry, until the train arrived and he could dispatch the gold to the territorial governor's office. He wished he could share his burden, but he was conscious of the fact that a secret shared was no longer a secret. There were two men in Jewel Creek in whom he had thought about confiding: Art Brown the owner of the general store, and Doc Henry Blue the Jewel Creek doctor. But, for the time being, he had decided to remain the sole custodian of the secret of Jewel Creek.

With each second seeming like an hour, it was going to be a long wait; an endless wait for a man on whom a mountain of trouble could come crashing down at any second in that long, sapping wait, if someone got the spark and grit to dislodge that first pebble.

Jewel Creek was a town with the beginnings of

rot, both moral and economic, and in Seth Benteen's experience of other towns, plenty of which he had drifted through, declining fortunes such as had beset Jewel Creek with the closing of a mine that had flattered to deceive, inevitably led to a break down in law and order. Honesty was something for folk who had a full belly and a feather bed and who spent their days trying to figure out how they would dispose of a surplus, rather than survive with a little. And although the seam of ore had suddenly run out only a month previously, already men who were upright then were now fighting and brawling as they sought solace in the saloon, unable to watch the increasingly gaunt faces round their tables. There was little point in telling them that they should use their dwindling resources to try and hold out until other work came along, because that was only advice that was listened to in a town where it was obvious that the lull was temporary.

Jewel Creek had the look and feel of a town that was past its time, and no amount of gab would convince anyone that it was otherwise. That's why, if folk knew that the crate in a cell in the jail held a quarter of a million dollars in gold and not farm implements, trouble would flare; trouble that Benteen, with only a part-time deputy who was on the verge of quitting and moving on before he lost the will to, could not contain.

'Hand in your badge, Seth,' Andy Black, the town smithy had advised only the day before. 'Make tracks like me, before this godforsaken town sucks you dry and you won't be left with the will to leave.'

Seth knew that Black's advice was good advice, and he was probably a fool not to take it, especially since the town had not been able to pay him a dime since the mine closed and the town's coffers quickly ran dry.

'Couldn't blame you if you upped and left, Seth,' Art Brown, the owner of the general store and chairman of the Town Council had told him. 'A man can't live on fresh air. But I'd take it as a personal favour if you'd tote your badge for as long as you can. Otherwise this town will become lawless.'

Seth Benteen did not need much persuading. Jewel Creek and Art Brown had been good to him. Two years previously, as down as any man could be after the death of his beloved wife Mary, he had blown into town destined for the saloon, as had been the case in too many towns back along the meandering trail he had ridden, thin and wasted and barely able to stay in his saddle.

That day there were a lot of hostile faces on the onlookers who paused on the boardwalks, most critical of the drifter riding in. Some found the voice to sling insults, and to tell him he was not wanted; that his kind had no place in a family town. But a strong voice rebuked those who berated him, a tall, gangling man with a nose that had been bent out of shape by a Yankee.

'Ain't you folks got any Christian charity?' he questioned those who would gladly see the back of the drifter, and not worry or care what might become of him. 'I was thirsty, you gave me to drink. I was hungry, you gave me to eat. I was naked and you clothed me. I was homeless and you took me in.'

The man was Art Brown. On that day, Seth Benteen's saviour.

As he headed for the saloon, his ambition to see clear glass at the bottom of another bottle of rotgut, Art Brown had cut his path.

'Are you going to make me a laughing stock, mister?' he had put to the drifter he'd just stood up for. 'Diving into the saloon like a no-good, when I've told folk that you've got worth enough to be bothered about!'

Seth Benteen remembered how he had come up short, changing his mind about forcing his way past the store-keeper into the saloon.

'A mangy dog's got more worth than me,' had been Benteen's impatient response; an impatience made all the keener by the fiery need for whiskey that had hellfire burning in his belly.

'He will have,' Art Brown said, 'if you step through those batwings, friend.'

Brown had stepped aside to let Benteen enter

the saloon, if that was his wish. To this day, he was not sure where he had drawn the strength from to resist his burning thirst, but he had turned away from the saloon and was on his way back to his scarecrow nag when Art Brown caught him up.

'Where're you headed, stranger?'

'Where I can get a drink without getting a damn lecture!' Benteen had replied grousily. 'A burg where there's no darn do-gooders to stop me!'

'Then I guess you're the saddlebum everyone reckons you are.' Art Brown turned and walked away. 'But if you're not,' he threw back over his shoulder, 'follow me.'

Brown entered the general store. Undecided between boarding his horse and riding out, or diving into the saloon, Seth Benteen had no intention of following the store-keeper. And then suddenly he was drawn to the general store, unable to understand why he had chosen the least attractive option.

There was an uncorked bottle of the finest Kentucky Rye open on the counter. Art Brown poured a generous drink. Benteen's innards quaked, and he reckoned that it would not take any great effort on his part to roll out his tongue across the floor to the glass of glistening amber liquor.

'Drink it,' the store-keeper invited.

'What's your game, mister?' Seth Benteen had flared angrily. 'I don't take kindly to being made

10

a fool of.'

'No man should,' Brown said. 'It's not my intention to humiliate you in any fashion, friend. I think you've got worth, you see.'

Reaching back over time, Seth Benteen's laughter now rang hollow in his ears.

'Worth, huh?' he'd scoffed.

'I figure,' Art Brown said. 'I ain't a man to waste my time.'

He shoved the glass of rye across the counter. Benteen's thirst exploded inside him, and the devil himself would not have kept him from the liquor. He slugged it down, and then came the shame.

'Had your fun?' he growled at Art Brown.

'I don't trade in another man's misfortune, mister,' the store owner had replied. 'Don't know when misfortune might come calling on me.' When Seth Benteen reached for the bottle of rye, Art Brown grabbed it. 'That, my friend,' he said with resolve, 'was your last drink. I don't employ drunks.'

'Employ?' Seth Benteen had yelped in surprise.

'That's what I said, mister. You ain't work shy, are you?'

'I'm a drifter, and a damn drunk,' Benteen growled, suspicious of the store-keeper's offer and motive. In his experience, a lot of hard-hearted bastards liked to build a man's hopes up before rubbing his nose in it, and belittle him out of some perverted sense of humour or righteousness. Any second now, if he took the bait, Brown would reel it in and a couple of his buddies would spring from the room just behind the counter to laugh their heads off. 'I don't know what game you're playing, mister,' he continued billigerently, 'but I ain't going to play it!'

Benteen had turned to walk out of the store when the door of the back room was yanked open just as he had anticipated that it would be. But it was not a friend of Art Brown's who put in a laughing appearance, but a young woman (probably the store-keeper's daughter by the likeness of features), spitting fire.

'You ungrateful hobo!' she berated Benteen. 'Uncle Art tried to pick you out of the gutter, and all you can do is insult him. If I had a horsewhip, I'd lay it on your back, mister.'

She swung around on her uncle.

'Maybe this will teach you a lesson, Uncle Art. And you'll stop trying to help every lame dog who puts in an appearance.'

'It's what the Good Lord asked us to do, Lucy,' the store-keeper gently rebuked his niece. 'In thanks for the good things He's given us.'

Lucy swung around on Seth Benteen, her pert nose twitching, her blue eyes aflame with scorn. 'Even the Lord must draw the line somewhere, Uncle Art!'

Seth Benteen had never felt so dressed down as

he had at that moment, wilting under the young woman's unflinching gaze.

'You musn't mind my niece,' Art Brown had said. 'She's got her ma's Irish temper.' He set his gaze on Benteen. 'I don't blame you for being suspicious of my offer, friend. I guess you've been kicked in the gut too many times to trust anyone. But my offer of work is genuine.' He held the drifter's eyes. 'As is my friendship.

'I own the grain store. The dollar you'll earn will be hard. I expect good work and fair work, and,' he emphasized, 'sober work, too. If you think you're up to it, you can start tomorrow morning at six sharp. It'll be sun-up to sun down. You can bunk down over the grain store. Ain't exactly palatial, but it's clean. Grub can be had from Mollie's Hash House along the street. Or you can get what you need and cook it yourself.'

'Uncle Art,' Lucy pleaded. 'He'll likely cut your throat for the dime in your pocket some night.'

Art Brown had sized Seth Benteen up long and hard before speaking again.

'I pride myself on getting the measure of a man, Lucy,' he had said. 'And I reckon that this man will come good, if given the chance.'

'How do you figure that,' Lucy wailed. 'If he was any good, he'd never have got himself the way he is to start with.'

'Your unkindness doesn't do you any credit, Lucy,' Art Brown berated his niece. He turned, stony-faced to Benteen. 'What's it going to be, mister? Hard work and decent living? Or slugging liquor and bumming round. Time to make up your mind.'

Seth Benteen recalled how, when he got over his suspicion and surprise, Art Brown's offer was the sweetest music his ears had heard in a long time.

'You've got yourself an employee, sir,' he told the store-keeper.

'You'll put your back into the work?' Brown checked.

'You bet, sir,' Seth had promised.

'I reckon you will at that,' the owner of the general store said, after lengthy consideration. He held out his hand. 'Art Brown's the name.'

Benteen pumped Art Brown's hand like a kid who'd got candy.

'Seth Benteen's my monicker,' he told Brown. 'And I'm mighty glad that I came to Jewel Creek, sir.'

'And this fiery filly is Lucy Brown, my late brother's daughter,' Brown introduced his niece.

Seth timidly offered his hand, and was glad he had not done so robustly when Lucy turned away, much to her uncle's annoyance.

'Can I talk to you, Uncle Art?' Lucy asked, and emphasized: 'Alone.'

'No need for behind the door gabbing, Lucy,' Art Brown said sternly. 'Seth is now part and parcel of this business.'

'It's not business I want to talk about!' Lucy snapped.

'Keep a civil tongue, young lady!' her uncle reacted.

'I'll mosey along outside,' Seth had offered. 'Let you folks jaw.'

From the boardwalk he could see, through the store window, Lucy in a heated disagreement with her uncle. And after a couple of minutes he went back inside the store just as Lucy Brown delivered her uncle an ultimatum.

'If he stays I go, Uncle Art.'

'No need to,' Benteen said. 'I won't be staying around, Mr Brown.' He rubbed his hand across his mouth like a man who had a godawful thirst. 'Your niece is right. I'm not fit to be with decent folk like you.'

'First hurdle and you're throwing in the towel,' Art Brown said, the disappointment in his voice bell clear.

'Did you expect it to be otherwise, Uncle Art?' Lucy piped up. 'The bottle will always win out with a drunk.'

'Thank you anyway,' Seth Benteen said to the store-keeper, and had slunk out of the general store and across the street to the saloon.

Art Brown watched him go, keenly disappointed.

'Read that fella wrong, I guess. Thought he had more grit.'

Lucy came and cuddled up to her uncle.

'You really will have to stop trying to help every lame dog that comes into town, Uncle Art. Now, I've been going through the books and we're showing a loss on that lumber you bought. And it's because, I reckon, that you've given away more free lumber to those settlers who rolled in last month than you've been paid for.'

'They're dirt poor, but honest, Lucy. They'll come good when they get on their feet.'

'By then you'll be out of house and home, if you're not careful,' Lucy Brown fretted.

The store owner put his arm round his niece's shoulders and hugged her fondly.

'We'll be just fine, Lucy,' he reassured her. 'Just fine.'

Lucy sighed.

'I just hope that you're not counting on the Archangel Gabriel arriving to bail you out, Uncle Art.'

Art Brown laughed, but his laughter was hollow, because just then the barkeep at the Silver Slipper Saloon ran Seth Benteen out of the watering-hole.

'We don't like whiskey-bummers round here,' he bellowed. 'Saddle tramps neither,' he added, his florid face made more flushed still by his anger. He lashed out a boot at the drifter, and sent him sprawling in the muddy street.

Men coming from the saloon to watch Benteen's

16

humiliation roared with laughter. Others on the boardwalk were more inhibited, but in the main in agreement with the saloon riff-raff.

'That's it, Lucy!' Art Brown declared. 'Seth Benteen is coming to work for me, no matter what you say or anyone else thinks!'

'Uncle Art,' Lucy wailed, as he hurried from the store.

'Save your breath, girl,' he flung back. 'I'm doing this, and that's that.'

'You're a stubborn old mule,' Lucy said.

'And you're an ornery young critter,' he responded with a chuckle.

Hurrying outside he helped Benteen to his feet.

'Ain't you folk got something better to do than enjoy a man's misfortune?' he rebuked the onlookers. He then turned his attention to the saloon men. 'I wouldn't expect anything else from whiskey-swilling trash like you!' he declared.

One of the men stepped forward, his hand hovering over his six-gun.

'If you weren't an old man, store-keeper . . .' He let the threat hang in the air.

'I figure you should apologize, mister,' his sidekick said, even more keen to use the .45 on his left hip, its walnut handle polished by frequent use.

The third man of the trio, trouble-seekers to a man, stepped forward. His preference was for the Bowie at his belt. Benteen had no doubt that the man could cut a fly going up a wall in half with the

17

wicked blade, and his keeness for trouble was even greater than his compatriots.

'It ain't right for you to favour a no-good saddle tramp in preference to decent folk, mister,' he growled.

Art Brown faced up to the man, foolishly so, in Seth Benteen's opinion. The store-keeper was no match for the opposition he was up against.

'I'm not interested in what you men think,' he said, stern-faced and unyielding. 'And I reckon that you're about as far from being decent folk as I am from the darn moon.'

The trouble-seeking trio exchanged ugly glances.

'That's real insultin', old man,' the knifeman snarled. 'Kinda says that our folks was no better than lowdown coyotes. Don't it, fellas?'

'Real insultin' to my sainted ma,' said the man who had first challenged Art Brown. 'I figure she'd expect me to protect her good name.'

Art Brown held open his coat.

'I'm unarmed.'

'Reckon it's a tad late to wriggle out, mister,' the knifeman scoffed. 'Ain't your brain got no control over your tongue?'

'That ain't no problem,' said the second man of the trio, unbuckling his gunbelt and tossing it to the store-keeper's feet. 'Now you have a gun, old man.'

The knifeman chuckled and sniffed the air.

'Wheweee!' he exclaimed. 'I think the oldster's just dirtied his pants, boys.'

'You leave my uncle be!'

Lucy Brown came from the store, rifle in hand.

'Well, I'll be blowed,' the knifeman said. 'Ain't she real purty, fellas?'

'The kinda woman a man could have a real good time with, Larry,' said Art Brown's first challenger.

'Ya know which end the bullets come from, Missy?' the second of the trio of hardcases mocked.

'You leave my niece be,' Art Brown pleaded. 'Your argument is with me.' He turned to Lucy. 'Get back inside, Lucy. Now, girl!'

'No, Uncle Art,' she said defiantly. 'I'm staying put.'

'I sure like a feisty woman, Benny,' said the knifeman, addressing the oldest of the trio.

Larry. That would be Larry Scott and Benny Creighton. And the third man would be Augie Sullivan. Collectively, the Creighton gang. The deadliest cut-throats in the territory, if not in the entire West.

Art Brown may as well have locked horns with Satan himself.

'Hold on now, fellas,' Augie Sullivan said. 'I figure that drawin' straws for first pleasure is only fair.'

'I'm the damn oldest,' Benny Creighton

snarled. 'And,' his small mean eyes fixed on Sullivan, 'the fastest with a gun. I reckon that gives me the longest straw, Augie.'

Sullivan held up his hands.

'Puttin' it that way, Benny,' he chuckled. 'I guess I ain't got no objection to second turn.' Larry Scott glared malevolently at Augie Sullivan, who shrugged philosophically. 'Or third.' He sneered. 'By then she should be nicely warmed up, I reckon.'

'Go inside, Lucy,' Art Brown pleaded, fearful for his niece.

'I ain't budging, Uncle Art,' Lucy Brown declared defiantly.

'Someone get the marshal,' the store-keeper pleaded with the people watching from the boardwalks.

'Al Bailey's out of town, Art,' a voice called out. 'Investigating the rustling out at the Bar Q ranch.'

'Then get his deputy,' Brown said.

The same voice answered.

'Randy's in bed with a fever.'

'Looks like all the aces in your deck have gone missin', old man,' Larry Scott sneered.

Art Brown picked up the gunbelt at his feet and, drawing himself up to his full height, he buckled on the gun, with fingers that seemed to have lost their touch.

'Ya know, fellas,' Benny Creighton snorted. 'I reckon we won't have to use lead at all. The old

20

man's goin' to drop dead from fright.'

With the .45 settled awkwardly on his right hip, in a fashion that told of Art Brown's unfamiliarity with a weapon, the store-keeper stood as tall as a man facing certain death could.

'Your fight is with me,' he said. 'I want your promise that the girl will be unharmed.'

'Sure.'

'Promise?' Brown asked.

'Surely,' Benny Creighton readily agreed, much to Art Brown's relief.

Seth Benteen was stunned by the store-keeper's naïvety.

'Benny's real good at keepin' promises, mister,' Augie Sullivan said. He shook his head. 'Only he don't remember so good.'

The trio laughed uproariously.

'Well, I guess it's 'bout time you licked my boots, old man,' Benny Creighton snarled.

'I've never licked any man's boots, mister,' Art Brown said defiantly. 'And I'm not going to start now.'

Creighton's anger flared.

'Then draw iron, old man,' he barked.

'My uncle is no gunnie,' Lucy Brown said. 'Killing him will be murder pure and simple.'

'Be careful, honey,' Larry Scott sneered. 'You'll have Benny cryin' in no time at all.'

'It's he who's the cause of the trouble!'

Seth Benteen recalled how small a man he felt

21

that day, beset by rotgut fever and unable to stand on legs that needed whiskey to give them false strength. To the day he'd die, he'd never forget the intensity of hatred and contempt that had burned in Lucy Brown's eyes. But her contempt of him had prodded his pride and he struggled shakily to his feet.

'She's right,' he croaked, the shake in his legs swiftly taking over his entire body. 'Your fight is with me.'

Benny Creighton swung his way.

'Are you challenging me, drunk?' he asked in disbelief.

'I guess that's what I'm doing, Creighton,' he had replied.

'Creighton?' a voice from the crowd cried. 'Benny Creighton?'

The killer swung round on the crowd, his features set in stone. 'Howdy, folks,' he growled. 'Any of you fine gents takin' exception to me bein' in town?' At first the crowd huddled, but as Larry Scott and Augie Sullivan lined up alongside Creighton, the crowd hurried away, all except one man. Benny Creighton glared at him.

'You sayin' I'm not welcome?' the gang leader barked.

'I'm saying that you're the scum of the earth, Creighton,' the man said.

Creighton stiffened.

'He's talking through his rear end,' Art Brown

said. 'Get back inside that office of yours, Henry,' the store-keeper urged. 'Pay him no heed, Creighton.'

Seth Benteen's gaze went to the shingle under which the man was standing. It read: HENRY BLUE MD.

'Run like the cowards you are!' Henry Blue berated the swiftly diminishing crowd. 'That's how scum like Creighton and his sidekicks poison decent towns.'

'Ya know, Benny,' Augie Sullivan chuckled. 'I reckon that when we're through, this town would be a good place to set up as an undertaker.'

'It's my fight, you ugly bastards,' Seth Benteen had spat.

He recalled now how darn scared he'd been, and how he regretted not having nurtured his gunskills, which had been considerable. But over a couple of years of slugging whiskey when and where he got it, his hands shook and his fingers had lost much of their flexibility. But he'd reckoned that day that it didn't matter much anyway. He was up against two of the toughest gunslick *hombres* in the territory in Augie Sullivan and Benny Creighton. And in Scott, he was facing a knifeman who could slit a fly's wings with a Bowie.

'He's mine, Benny,' Augie Sullivan had said, stepping off the saloon porch into the street, his face twisted with hatred.

Creighton leaned against an overhang support beam, and took the makings to roll a smoke from his vest pocket.

'Right between the eyes, Augie,' he sneered.

'How about through his left eye before he blinks, Benny?' Sullivan said.

'You're not that good, Augie,' Larry Scott snorted. 'Now, I figure that I could pluck out that eye with a knife.'

Augie Sullivan sneeringly dismissed Scott's claim.

'Be interestin' to see, that,' Creighton said.

'You said he was mine,' Sullivan protested to Creighton.

'So I've changed my mind, Augie,' the gang-leader flung back.

The flare-up between the gang members that Seth Benteen had been hoping for, fizzled out, Augie Sullivan thinking better of challenging Creighton. Now Scott stepped forward with the swagger of a man who had no doubt about his ability to do what he had boasted he could do.

'I'll even leave the knife in its sheath, drunk, until you clear leather,' he said. 'Don't want folk to say that this was an unfair fight.'

Seth Benteen turned to Art Brown.

'I'm sorry that helping me brought trouble to your door and to this town, Mr Brown,' he apologized. 'But I'm sure mighty pleased that you saw fit to try and help me, sir.'

'You don't stand a chance, Benteen,' Art Brown pleaded. 'Money,' he proposed to Benny Creighton. 'How much to leave town right now?'

The gang-leader's interest perked up.

'Money, huh?' He nodded in Benteen's direction. 'How much do you reckon the saddlebum is worth, mister?'

'Not a damn cent!' Benteen had said. 'Sorry, Mr Brown. But I ain't for buying like a slave.' He squared up to Scott. 'Ready when you are.'

Larry Scott looked to Benny Creighton, who shrugged philosophically.

'I guess we can just take what we want from this burg anyway,' he said. 'Kill him, Larry.'

To the present day, Seth Benteen could not explain the lifting of the fog from his liquor-sozzled brain. Or the energy that powered into his right hand, loosening muscles that had, seconds before, been stiff and inflexible.

In his better days, he had been reasonably fast. But on this day, his speed had astonished him and, more importantly, Larry Scott. Scott's second of surprise had been enough to give Benteen the edge. His bullet blasted a ragged hole in Scott's chest, and he fell forward on his own knife, not that it mattered, he was already dead.

Benny Creighton dived for his gun. A second shot from Benteen's gun took a chunk out of the overhang support beam against which the gang-

25

leader had been lounging. The chunk of wood sped along his right cheek, tearing a deep furrow in the flesh. Augie Sullivan thought about going for his gun, but Art Brown had him covered.

'Looks like you fellas have outstayed your welcome,' the store-keeper piped up, relishing the lightning quick turn of events. 'We're civilized folk in Jewel Creek. You boys hit the trail. We'll bury your comrade.'

Sullen and hate-filled, Benny Creighton mounted up, nursing the wound on his cheek. His hatred was exclusively directed at Seth Benteen.

'This ain't the end of this, mister,' he promised.

Mounting up alongside Creighton, Augie Sullivan expressed a similar view.

'We'll settle accounts one day,' he growled. 'Of that you can be certain, friend.'

As they rode out of town under threat of Brown and Benteen's guns, folk began to re-emerge from wherever they had taken refuge, cock-a-hoop, now that the threat to their well-being had vanished.

'Darn, Benteen,' Art Brown exclaimed. 'We make a pretty good team.'

'Hah!'

Both men turned to Lucy Brown, whose scorn, Benteen recalled, was even greater.

'What the heck's wrong with you, niece?' the store-owner wanted to know.

Lucy Brown shook her blonde head, her blue

eyes contemptuous.

'Not alone did you risk your life for a drunk, Uncle Art,' she rebuked Brown. 'But he's a gunfighter, too.'

'I'm no gunfighter,' Benteen had corrected.

'If you're not, you're sure not far from being one,' Lucy threw back.

Goaded and anxious for some loco reason to redeem himself in Lucy Brown's eyes, Seth had blurted out. 'A badge-toter has to be gun-handy. As slick as the man he has to square up to.'

'You were a lawman?' Art Brown asked, amazed.

'Used to be,' Benteen had confirmed. His eyes took on a misty sadness. 'A long time ago, when times were better than they are now, Mr Brown.'

'Heck, drop the Mr, Seth. Call me Art.

'You're downright hopeless, Uncle Art,' Lucy Brown wailed, and stormed off to the general store.

'She'll come round, Seth,' Brown said confidently.

It surprised Seth Benteen that he hoped she would.

'Follow me, Seth.' The store-owner pointed along the street. 'The grain store is this way.'

Now, two years on, having become the Marshal of Jewel Creek, sitting on a quarter of a million dollars and the headaches that brought with it, Seth Benteen might be excused for thinking that Art Brown had done him no favours by giving

27

him a job in his grain store in the first place, and then persuading the Town Council of his worthiness to become the Marshal of Jewel Creek a year ago.

CHAPTER TWO

Benteen looked behind him at the cell holding the so-called crate of farm implements and wondered who the stash belonged to, and why it had been dispatched in the way it had. And, of course, he also wondered about its source and its purpose. The crate was marked: Farm Implements, as were four other crates he'd come across, but unlike those crates, it bore no delivery address. Jewel Creek was close to the Mexican border, and Benteen had heard rumours of illegal gun shipments across the Rio Grande. Gun-running was a very profitable trade, because there were always wars and threats of war. There was even a rumour that a clandestine group of former Civil War officers, both Southern and Yankee, called the Freedom Brotherhood, would prefer the United States to be run more to their liking, and were, it was said, prepared to take up arms to enforce their will which was, again as rumour would have it, far removed from the democratic model of government which Americans were priviliged to live under. Could the $250,000 be payment for the weapons they'd need? Mexico and further into South America were prime sources for illegal arms. And indeed, a group in America who sought to impose their will would find many fellow-travellers in places like Mexico. Heresay, and Benteen hoped that that was all it was, spoke of a grand alliance between the tyrants ruling Mexico and the revolutionary movement in the United States of the Freedom Brotherhood. Such an alliance would of course be treasonable, but when the stakes were high, and there was no higher stake than the control of America, men would be prepared to risk their immortal souls for such a prize.

No one knew the identity of the men who formed the Freedom Brotherhood, but word had it that they were an unstable mix of religious zealots and the disillusioned; men with gripes and moans, who would steer the United States on a course that was certain to end in disaster, rather than fulfilling the promise of the new post-Civil War country. Some said that men who were at the very centre of government supported the Brotherhood's aims, and treacherously aided and abetted their cause, while masquerading as democrats.

The tyrannical Mexican government would

welcome the success of the Freedom Brotherhood and, it was said, actively supported it. The Mexican peasants were looking across the Rio Grande at the swift progress of their fledgling neighbour, and longed for its freedoms of equality and free speech, and the franchise of the ballot box. The Mexican Grandees saw the danger of such longing to their priviliged positions, were the model of the United States to be repeated in Mexico.

The Freedom Brotherhood would no doubt call themselves patriots, but to Seth Benteen's way of thinking a patriot was a man who accepted the will of the people, expressed fairly. The Brotherhood sought to impose rather than agree. Only the previous month a US marshal who had been on the trail of gun-runners was strung up as a warning to others who might be of a mind to follow in his footsteps. There was no clear evidence that the Freedom Brotherhood had directly committed the atrocity. But they were guilty and complicit in creating a climate where such atrocities would occur. The leaders of the Brotherhood might have high-faluting if misplaced ideas and loyalties, but their cause would attract the lower forms of life that inevitably attached themselves to such a cause, for profit or simply for murderous mayhem.

These were dangerous times. America was raw and bleeding after the Civil War, rife with suspicions and hatred. A melting pot of views and opinions that was ever-changing, making it difficult for its citizens to know right from wrong. Good from bad. Wise from foolish. In fact the ideal climate existed for mayhem.

Seth Benteen wished that he had never ridden out to help the former marshal, who had given up the badge to set up a horse ranch. Along with Art Brown, it was Al Bailey's endorsement that had swung the Town Council vote in his favour.

If he had not ridden out to Walnut Creek where Bailey had his ranch, he would never have come across the wagon with the busted wheel. He would never have found the crate full of gold. And he would never have inherited the headache he had.

He glanced up at the wall clock. It read: 1.30 a.m. It was going to be a heck of a long night. Footsteps on the boardwalk outside the law-office had Benteen sitting bolt upright.

CHAPTER THREE

The Jewel Creek marshal's hand dropped to his sixgun as the footsteps paused outside the law office door. He had not confided in anyone about the treasure he was the keeper of, but that did not mean that he was the only one with knowledge of its existence. The crate's destination could have been Jewel Creek, or one of a couple of towns not too distant. It could also have been headed across the Rio to Mexico, or for delivery to the secret camps in the hills and mountains there had been talk of, being made ready as bases from which to launch the Freedom Brotherhood's uprising. There might even be a wing of the secret society right on his doorstep.

'Now there's a heck of a worrying thought,' Benteen murmured.

His was a lonely watch and a heavy burden. Benteen had sought out Art Brown to confide in, reckoning that his secret would be safe with Jewel

Creek's most upright citizen, but Lucy had told him that he had business to attend to in Hadley Wells, a town about fifteen miles south of Jewel Creek, nearer the border. A prosperous neighbour, Brown had spoken to Seth Benteen about moving his business to Hadley Wells, seeing no future in Jewel Creek.

'Hadley Wells is about as close to Mexico as you can get,' had been the marshal's reaction. 'Without being in Mexico proper.'

'You don't think the move makes sense?' Brown had asked.

'Why not Bohane Junction?' had been his response. 'That would seem by far a better and safer choice than Hadley Wells. If trouble flares between the US and Mexico, which it likely will if the Mexes keep poking their noses into US business and fermenting trouble by supporting outfits like the Freedom Brotherhood, Hadley Wells will be right in the firing line, I reckon.'

Art Brown laughed.

'Darn, Seth. You don't believe all that rubbish about an attempt to overthrow the government, do you?' he asked, shaking his head in disbelief.

'You can't deny that there's a whole passel of critters whose noses are out of joint after the Civil War, Art.'

'All wars bring their hotheads and malcontents who gripe and groan,' Brown said. 'But that's a long way from revolution.'

'So you don't think the Brotherhood exists, then?'

The store-keeper shook his head vigorously.

'I reckon that it's the tallest yarn ever told, Seth. Now about moving to Hadley Wells with Lucy and me.'

'I reckon that Lucy wouldn't want me cluttering up any move, Art,' had been Benteen's honest opinion.

'Oh, she'll thaw, Seth,' the store-owner promised. 'I've seen the signs.'

'Well, all I've got to say to that, Art, is that your eyesight must be a whole lot better than mine,' he groaned.

'Lucy will come round,' Brown said confidently. 'So are you coming to Hadley Wells? This town's finished, Seth. Hadley Wells is a thriving town. It'll be a city one day soon, I reckon, needing strong law.'

Brown's talk of abandoning Jewel Creek, of which he was one of the founding fathers, had surprised Benteen, and he had been unable to hide his astonishment.

'You think I'm running out, don't you, Seth?' he'd said. 'A rat leaving a sinking ship.'

'Every man has to make up his own mind, Art,' the marshal said. 'But I think it's early days yet to give up on Jewel Creek. I reckon that once the shock of the mine folding is over, men will look for new ways to make the town viable. I'm not saying

35

that it will ever match the grandeur of Hadley Wells. But maybe that will be all to the good in the long run. If the West is to grow and prosper it will need family towns, the kind of town that Jewel Creek was, only a short couple of months ago. Hadley Wells ain't that. I hear it's as close to being an open town as don't matter. Full of cut-throats and intrigue.'

'It's a new town. All new towns have growing pains. It'll settle down.' Frustrated, Art Brown pointed out, 'I'm a businessman, Seth, and there's no business in Jewel Creek. And I'm not sure that I can wait around for it to pick up again, if it ever does.'

He frowned.

'And I've got Lucy's future to consider,' he'd said with finality.

'And what does Lucy have to say about all of this?'

'She likes the idea, Seth.'

'Likes the idea, huh?' the marshal said, mournfully.

'Surprises you, huh.'

'To tell the truth, you could knock me down with a feather, Art. I figured Lucy to be a dyed-in-the-wool citizen of Jewel Creek.'

'Knocked me back too, when she so readily agreed to the idea when I mooted it a couple of weeks ago. Until I thought of Charles Barrington . . .'

36

'Charles Barrington?'

'Yes,' Brown confirmed. 'A lawyer in Hadley Wells. Has come here on business a couple of times recently, and sweet-talked Lucy it seems.'

'You mean Lucy and Barrington are a pair?'

'Danced every dance together at Ned Drake's barn dance last month. I was in bed, ailing, so I wasn't there to see all of this closeness between Lucy and Charles. But when I suggested the move to Hadley Wells, Lucy jumped at the idea like a fish snatching at flies in a creek.'

'Is that a fact,' Benteen said, as cheerily as he could, while his heart ached.

Seth Benteen had hoped that in time Lucy's attitude to him would soften when she saw him come good, but now he saw what a fool's wish that had been. The fact was that even if Lucy had looked on him more kindly, Art Brown saw Lucy's future with a man of substance, and not the wife of a man whose future was as precarious as a one-legged dancer.

'Think about moving to Hadley Wells, Seth,' Art Brown urged.

'I like it fine right here, Art,' had been his reply.

'I guess the decision is yours to make, Seth,' the store-keeper said, genuinely regretful. 'But I reckon you're making the wrong decision. Hadley Wells is bursting at the seams with opportunities for a man to make good. I've got powerful friends there. Men who see the future of this country with sparkling clear vision. Come along, Seth.'

Benteen glanced down at the star on his chest.

'You have been good to me, Art,' he'd said. 'But I took an oath to uphold the law. And I figure that pretty soon I'll be called on to honour that oath to the full.'

'You've got a deputy to fill your boots,' the store-keeper pointed out.

Benteen shook his head.

'Andy Cleary's already decided to quit town.'

'Sensible,' was Brown's opinion. 'A dying town will suck the life out of you if you stay. Until you won't have the will left to leave.'

'I'll take my chances, Art,' Benteen replied. 'If that's OK with you?'

The marshal's reverie was interrupted as the door of the office began to open. Seth Benteen was relieved when Doc Henry Blue poked his head round the door.

'Howdy, Doc,' the marshal warmly greeted Blue, much relieved. He checked the wall clock. 'You're out late, Henry.'

'Just dropped by to jaw some, Seth,' Blue said. 'If you don't mind. These days, sleep visits infre-quently.'

Henry Blue was a widower who had adored his wife and lived every minute of every day just for her. When Martha Blue died, the doc was set adrift in a world that was alien to him, and for a time he had sought solace in whiskey. It was a common thread that held them together.

'Just can't stand being in the house without Martha, Seth,' he had confided to him, one night Benteen had had him as a guest in the jail. 'Every inch of the place reminds me of her. I know it can't be, not after two years, but I can still smell Martha's perfume, Seth.'

That night, Seth had listened long into the small hours of the morning as Henry Blue rambled on. And after that, on the marshal's invitation, the town doctor had become a regular visitor to the law office, staying until he ran out of wind and memories, mostly the memories he had related on his previous visit. Often the doc would remain on as Seth's guest for the night.

'Some day you might want to unburden yourself, Seth,' he'd say on leaving the next morning. 'If that day ever comes, I'm hear to listen.'

Seth Benteen wondered if right now might be the time to do just that – unburden himself about what was really in the box of so-called farm implements in a cell behind the marshal's office.

CHAPTER FOUR

Henry Blue was no fool. It took no time at all for him to shrewdly guess what was weighing so heavily on Seth Benteen's mind.

'Would that wooden crate I saw you haul through the rear door a couple of hours ago have anything to do with those drooping shoulders you've taken on, Seth?'

'Crate, Henry?' the marshal hedged.

'You ain't fooling old Henry Blue none with that innocent dial, Seth. I couldn't sleep. Took a walk to settle me down. Passing the general store, I saw a wagon turn into the alley alongside the jail. Now I'm a curious cuss, Seth. Moseyed along to see what a wagon was doing back of the jail late at night. Saw you drag a crate into the jail, and it was mighty hard work, Seth. Now if you haven't got the Holy Grail in there, it's the next nearest thing.'

'You're talking cow dung, Henry. All that's in that box are farm implements. It's right there on the side of the crate, plain to see.'

Henry Blue raised an extraordinarily bushy eyebrow for a man with almost no facial hair.

'You're not fooling old Henry Blue, Seth,' he chuckled. 'I figure that what it says on the outside of the crate isn't what it's got inside. Because no one goes to the trouble you've gone to for a box of spades and hoes.'

'Gold, Henry,' Benteen said resignedly, but grateful at last that he could share the secret that had been weighing him down since early that afternoon.

The Jewel Creek doctor's eyes popped.

'Gold?' he said in a hoarse whisper. 'A whole crateful of gold?'

Seth Benteen nodded.

Henry Blue's next question was an obvious one.

'How did you come by it, Seth?'

'This afternoon, I rode out to Al Bailey's to lend a helping hand. He ain't as perky as he used to be since his horse threw him a couple of months ago. There was a remuda of wild horses in a canyon south of the ranch he wanted to round up. On my way back I came across a wagon in Corkrell's Creek. It had busted a wheel, and the driver was real excited. I told him that I'd send help from town when I got back, but that suggestion made him even more excited. Just then the reason for his anxiety became clear. The couple of spokes that were intact, gave way and the wagon tilted, pitching that crate back there,' he pointed over his shoulder to the jail, 'into the creek. It busted open, and my eyes popped at what fell out.

'On seeing the busted crate, the wagon driver grabbed his chest, croaked and dropped dead.'

'That's the fella you brought to town. Said you found him out on the trail. No knife or bullet wounds, so you figured he had died of natural causes.'

'That bit was true,' the marshal said.

'So what're you going to do now?' Blue asked, his faded grey eyes positively glowing with excitement. 'I mean, with the gold?'

'Putting it on the noon train for the governor's office in the territorial capital.'

Henry Blue's astonishment was one hundred per cent genuine.

'Isn't that a tad foolish, Seth? What if the train is held up? I hear Benny Creighton busted out of prison and joined up with his old partners. He'll be wanting cash in his saddle-bags. And they'll be heading this way, I figure, for Creighton to keep his promise to even the score with you after that bust up you two had a couple of years ago.

'You should be swearing in a couple of deputies, and not concerning yourself with that gold.'

'I have to get the gold out of town, Henry. Can you imagine what kind of trouble would beset the town if folk found out about it?'

Henry Blue shook his head vigorously.

'Don't see any danger. This is a law-abiding town, Seth.'

'Used to be,' Benteen stated. 'When men were able to fill their wives and children's bellies. With the mine gone, they're desperate men, and desperate men are dangerous men, Henry.'

'I reckon, Seth,' the Jewel Creek doctor conceded.

'Once the gold is on the train, I'll telegraph the governor's office that it's on its way. After that, if it's stolen, well that ain't nothing to do with me. Unless, of course, the Creighton gang holds up the train in my jurisdiction. Then I'll have to hunt the no-good cut-throats down.'

'Only one thing wrong with all of that,' Henry Blue said, after a thoughtful pause.

'And what might that be?' the marshal enquired.

'Once you send that wire about the gold being on the train, every critter in these parts will know about it. There's no way that Abe Harrington the telegraphist will keep his big mouth shut.'

'That's true, Henry,' the Jewel Creek lawman admitted, but his smile was foxy. 'But you see Abe will never know that he's sending a telegraph about gold.'

'How do you figure that?' the doc wanted to know.

'Simple, Henry,' the marshal said. 'I've got a friend in the governor's office. A fella by the name of Frank Clinton, who wore the blue of the Union with me. We used to use a codename for really important freight. Once I wire him that Golden Eagle is coming his way, he'll know that it's a shipment of gold. That's the code we used in the war for shipping gold, you see.'

'That's very clever, Seth,' Henry Blue complimented Benteen. 'But can you trust this fella?'

'I'd trust Frank Clinton with my life, Henry,' Seth Benteen stated unequivocally.

'Have you heard about the Freedom Brotherhood, Seth?' Blue asked. 'Revolutionaries. A group of men who'd run this country very differently.'

'I've heard stories. And maybe that's all they are, Henry. Tall-tales told round camp-fires and in saloons.'

'Don't reckon so, Seth,' the doc said determindly. 'Word has it that a lot of very important men, some in the government itself, are part of the Freedom Brotherhood. I can't help but fret that maybe this Frank Clinton might be one of them. Can you imagine how many guns a crateful of gold would buy?' he asked wide-eyed.

'Probably enough to start a revolution, you reckon?' Seth speculated.

'Maybe you should hold on to the gold,' Blue suggested.

'I can't do that, Henry,' the Jewel Creek lawman stated bluntly. 'I'm a man alone.'

44

'Swear in a couple of deputies.'

'If I hire deputies, even if the town could pay them, which it can't, everyone would know about the gold. The men I'd hire would probably cut my darn throat and heist it.'

Henry Blue shook his head soulfully.

'You've surely got yourself a brain-busting dilemma, Seth,' he sighed. 'The town could surely do with that kind of windfall.' Seth Benteen had an uneasy moment, trying to figure out if he had made a mistake in taking the doc into his confidence. 'Don't fret, Seth,' he said, shrewdly guessing the marshal's concerns. 'My lips are sealed.'

Marshal Seth Benteen's apprehension eased a little, but not a great deal. Henry Blue was a man who was fighting a fondness for liquor, and that was one problem he fully understood. Blue hadn't touched a drop in weeks, but the demons still rode his back. Now Benteen worried that those demons might win out. Henry Blue, sober, was a man of the utmost discretion; however, Henry Blue, liquored up, could not hold his tongue.

Had he been unwise and foolish in the extreme to share his secret with the town doctor?

CHAPTER FIVE

Henry Blue returned to speculating about the Freedom Brotherhood.

'You reckon that maybe this gold belongs to the Freedom Brotherhood, Seth? I've heard stories about the Brotherhood being in cahoots with the Mexicans.'

'I've heard those stories too, Henry,' the marshal said. 'And that would be treason, I figure.'

'You reckon, Seth?'

'Surely do, Doc,' Benteen said, unequivocally.

'So you'd sling any man in the Brotherood in jail for treason?'

'Treason's a hanging offence, Henry,' the marshal stated bluntly. 'We've been through hell. Another war ain't going to make this country any better. I say that it's now time to heal those wounds instead of opening new wounds.'

'You figure that there's anyone in Jewel Creek in the Brotherhood?'

'It's a secret Brotherhood. No one knows who's in or out.' Benteen chuckled. 'Heck, you could be one of the Freedom Brotherhood, Henry.'

'Wouldn't that be really something, Seth,' he said, the marshal laughing along with him. 'And you just after telling me about all that gold you've got stashed.'

Seth Benteen kept laughing, but his laughter was now masking his worry. He'd just stated the fact that the Freedom Brotherhood, being a secret organization, no one knew the identity of its members, and he'd just blabbered to Henry Blue.

What if the Jewel Creek doctor was a member of the Brotherhood? He had not criticized the Brotherhood the way most men who were committed to building the United States did. Blue had asked him if he reckoned that there were any members of the Brotherhood in Jewel Creek? Had that been an innocent question? Or might it be that the doc was fishing for any information he might have?

Seth Benteen could not believe that Henry Blue would be a traitor. But then by the very nature of treason, traitors soon learned the skills of seeming to be the opposite to what they really were. Henry Blue's next speculation did nothing to ease Benteen's worry.

'Have you thought that maybe the gold was for delivery to someone in Jewel Creek, Seth?'

'The thought did cross my mind, Henry,' the lawman said. 'But the natural dropping point for a shipment of farm implements, if the ruse was to be maintained right to the end, and I can't see any reason why it shouldn't be, would be the hardware store.' Benteen shook his head dismissively. 'Art Brown owns the hardware store. And I figure that a man would travel a long way before he'd cross paths with one more honest, upright and loyal as Art.'

Henry Blue raised his eyebrows and puckered his lips.

'The perfect front for a man embarked on treachery, wouldn't you say, Seth?'

Seth Benteen was not ready to change his opinion of Art Brown, but he had to admit to the veracity of Henry Blue's thinking.

'That's the most loco idea I ever heard,' the marshal pronounced. 'I reckon no one in this town is more of a patriot than Art Brown.'

'I guess to you, Art's God Almighty, Seth,' the doc grinned.

'I owe no man more than I do Art Brown, Henry,' Benteen declared sincerely.

'Thought for a while you'd be Art's nephew-in-law.'

'What put that crazy idea in your head? Lucy Brown never took, and will never take a shine to me, Henry.'

'That's not what Art told me.'

Seth Benteen perked up. 'What did he tell you, Doc?'

'Said that Lucy's bluster was down to her not wanting to admit to herself or anyone else that she has a hankering for you. But I guess you were too darn slow to cotton on, Seth. Now your chance is gone. Charles Barrington, Art's probable nephew-in-law, has arrived in town from Hadley Wells.' Seth Benteen's pleasure at hearing what Henry Blue had said about Lucy's hankering for him, a view that had knocked him sideways, died a death on hearing about the arrival in Jewel Creek of Charles Barrington. 'Maybe even at this late hour, you'd admit to yourself and tell Lucy that you're in love with her, Seth.'

The marshal jumped up from his chair.

'I do declare, Henry Blue,' he ranted. 'You get the funniest notions!'

'So you're just going to sit and do nothing?' Blue challenged. 'While Barrington steals the prettiest woman in Jewel Creek and for many a mile beyond, right from under your nose.'

'There's nothing to do!' Benteen growled.

Henry Blue stood up, took his hat from the marshal's desk and put it on, vainly looking in the mirror on the wall behind Benteen to get the angle of the headgear right.

'I guess it's Lucy's intended husband who has persuaded Art to move to Hadley Wells, wouldn't you say, Seth?'

49

'I guess.'

'Art says that he asked you along?'

'He did.'

'Why do you think he did that?' Henry Blue asked.

'Said that Hadley Wells would soon be a city, and they'd need a good lawman.'

'You're one dumb critter, Seth Benteen,' the doc chuckled. 'Don't you see, Art wants you where Lucy will be.'

'Like I said, Henry,' the Jewel Creek lawman snorted. 'You get the funniest notions in that head of yours.'

Shaking his head, Henry Blue went to the law office door and paused before opening it, his shrewd eyes locking with the marshal's.

'You know what I figure, Seth. No one will come looking to claim that gold.'

'You figure, Henry?'

The Jewel Creek doctor now gave voice to Benteen's own thoughts.

'Because, my friend, whoever shipped it in the first place under the guise of farm implements, wanted that gold for reasons that the law would not agree with. Like the purchasing of guns.'

'The Freedom Brotherhood?' the marshal speculated.

Henry Blue did not answer his question, if it needed answerng in the first place.

' 'Night, Seth.'

When Henry Blue left, Benteen sat quietly thoughtful, mulling over the doc's question about members of the Freedom Brotherhood in town. And although he could not think of any likely candidates, the fact was that were it so, it would be logical. Jewel Creek was not far from the Mexican border by normal route, and even less distant by the myriad of trails through the hills used by outlaws criss-crossing back and forth into Mexico; the same trails over which guns could be smuggled. Many of the trails were treacherous, falling into disrepair due to lack of use or from the ravages of inclement weather. So that meant that up-to-the-minute knowledge would be needed to safely smuggle weapons from Mexico, the kind of knowledge that a local would have. Otherwise a valuable cargo could be lost on a trail that might disintegrate under the weight of a wagon carrying guns, pitching into a ravine or canyon, and even if recovered, would likely be damaged beyond repair. Some folk said that the Freedom Brotherhood were almost ready to begin their revolt. That a full battalion of the Mexican Army were on standby to cross the Rio Grande the second the signal was given to be partners in the revolution.

He'd be damn glad when that train arrived and he could ship the gold out to the governor's office, because he did not agree with Henry Blue's idea that no one would come looking for the gold. His belief was that they were already searching high and low for it. And if it was the property of the Freedom Brotherhood, the search would be even more frantic and more deadly, because they needed those guns. Otherwise believers in their cause, tiring of bluster, would begin to drift away, thinking that talk of revolution was nothing more than huff and puff.

The marshal tensed as he heard a scratching at the back door of the jail, so slight that in normal times it would have gone unnoticed. Could this be the trouble that he feared was on the way?

CHAPTER SIX

Seth Benteen winced as the chair he was seated on creaked when he stood up. He paused, crouched, listening for any sign that the chair's creak had been heard by whoever was trying to break in through the back door. The stillness was eerie. Did that mean that the creak of the chair had been heard and the interlopers had fled? Or was it just a natural break in their attempts to break in. He went to quench the lamp on his desk, but thought better of it. He would lower it only. And then he changed his mind about that too, because there could be someone watching the law-office, and if the lamp went out or its glow was lowered, it would signal to the watcher that the marshal was wise to trouble and was ready to meet it.

There it was again. The scratching. Whoever the intruder might be, he was not an expert in picking locks. The lock on the back door of the jail was sturdy, but no work of genius. The most amateur picker would have its mechanism tumbling in seconds. Had he slid the bolt home, he wondered? Being a cautious man, he probably had. But he could not be certain. Gingerly, testing the boards before he stepped on them, he crept to the edge of the door that led to the cells. Luckily he had left the door open. Otherwise, the first he might have known of the interlopers was when they popped up in front of him in the law office proper.

He edged his way slowly along the narrow hall past the cells to the back door of the jail, still testing every floorboard before he stepped on it. The flicker of the lamp at the end of the narrow passage sent dancing shadows up the walls. It had burned low, and its light, not great, added an eerie feel to Benteen's ponderous progress. As he made his way, a thought that was nagging at the edges of his mind went from mere possibility to likely probability. The scratching at the back door might be a ruse to get him out of the law office, and allow the interlopers admission that way. As the silence intensified, the probability of that happening heightened. He was a man caught between two options, which amounted to a rock and a hard place. And all he could hope for was that he had chosen the right course of action. But he was growing more and more conscious of the fact that when Henry Blue had left, he had not locked the front door!

He slid his sixgun from its holster and prepared to yank open the back door of the jail.

In another part of town, four men sat huddled together, their faces drawn with worry. They were the Jewel Creek Chapter of the Freedom Brotherhood. They had been gathered for over an hour in an extreme state of anxiety, waiting for news about the gold shipment that had gone missing; gold they sorely needed to pay the gun-smugglers who were waiting in the hills outside of town. These were men of quick-temper and ruthless disposition, and they would not take kindly to having hauled arms all the way from Mexico with no profit at the end of their journey. They had no interest in, or loyalty to, the aspirations of the Brotherhood, theirs was simply a mission of self-enrichment. And if their plans to that end were thwarted, they might very well seek revenge on those who had not held to their part of the devil's bargain that had been struck in Hadley Wells the previous month. Footsteps on the boardwalk outside the parlour window had the sweating men sitting upright in their chairs. The footsteps paused. The front door of the house opened, and the footsteps came along the hall to the parlour. The parlour door opened, and the man whom they hoped had good news for them stepped into the room.

'Have you found out where the gold is?' one of

the waiting men asked the Chapter Leader.

'Yes,' he answered.

The men's relief was palpable.

'Where is it?' a second man asked eagerly.

The Chapter Leader chuckled.

'In the jail,' he said. Puzzled, the men looked at their leader. 'Marshal Benteen came across it and is kindly minding it for us.'

The first man who had spoken, spoke again.

'Benteen? Minding gold for the Freedom Brotherhood?' His voice reeked of disbelief.

'Sidney's right,' another of the men said. 'Benteen would run us all into jail if he knew we were members of the Freedom Brotherhood.'

'How the hell did he come by it?' another man asked.

'This afternoon, the marshal rode out to Al Bailey's ranch to help him rope some wild horses. On his way back, he came across Devine, stuck in a creek with a busted wheel. The crate carrying the gold fell off the wagon and broke open. Devine got a heart attack when that happened. Benteen hid the gold, and brought it into town under cover of darkness tonight. It's stashed in the jail, waiting to be picked up.'

The second man who had spoken earlier made another point.

'If anyone else in this town knows about the gold, it could be hijacked,' he fretted.

The Chapter Leader chuckled.

'No one but me and Benteen knows,' he reassured his co-conspirators.

'Are you sure about that?' the fourth man of the Chapter asked, speaking for the first time.

'I'm certain,' the Chapter Leader said.

'So what comes next?' he questioned the Chapter Leader.

'We'll go and get the gold, of course.'

'You think that Seth Benteen will just let us walk in and take it?' the man called Sidney snorted.

'We kill Benteen if necessary,' was the Chapter Leader's chilling reply.

'We haven't got much time,' the first man who had spoken said. 'That gold is supposed to be in the hills by tomorrow to pay for the guns.'

'It only takes a couple of seconds to kill a man. After that, we'll load up the gold and Ned Blake will haul it to where the gun-smugglers will be waiting to trade.' His eyes glistened feverishly. 'Shortly this country will have the kind of government that will not tolerate any opinions.' He grinned. 'Except the ones the Brotherhood agrees with, of course. Now,' he strolled to a drinks cabinet at the far side of the parlour, 'it's chilly out tonight, so let's have ourselves a whiskey before we go and take possession of our gold.'

Drinking their whiskies, the Chapter Leader said, 'Imagine, in a couple of days the Brotherhood will be rising throughout the length and breadth of this country, following on our example.' He held up his glass in salute. 'To the Freedom Brotherhood, gentlemen!'

'The Freedom Brotherhood,' they chorused.

'One . . . Two . . .' Marshal Seth Benteen muttered. 'Three!'

He yanked open the back door of the jail.

CHAPTER SEVEN

There was no one there. The Jewel Creek marshal looked cautiously into the dark alley, trying to look every which way at once, conscious of the fact that one clip of a gunbutt and the stash of gold would have vanished when he'd come to. The alley was deserted. But Seth Benteen's worries were far from over. The scratching at the jail door probably meant that someone, other than the trustworthy Henry Blue, knew of the treasure he was hiding. Who could that someone be? He tried to shun his next thought, but it demanded consideration, ugly as it was. The only one he had shared his secret with had been the Jewel Creek doctor. Could it be that Henry Blue had betrayed his confidence? Unimaginable as that was, a second ugly thought was added to the first. Might Henry Blue be a member of the Freedom Brotherhood?

Preoccupied with his thoughts, the marshal almost leapt out of his skin when he saw eyes looking at him from the dark, until the mongrel he had taken to feeding a couple of days previously ambled forward, head low, looking whupped and sorry for himself. He leaned to examine the lower part of the door more closely and laughed at his own foolishness when he saw scratch marks consistent with the mongrel's long, uncared for claws. He patted the mongrel's cowed head.

'Come on inside,' the marshal said. 'I think I can scrounge up some morsels, dog.'

Excited by the warmth of the lawman's reception, the mongrel jostled with him as they made their way back along the narrow passage to the marshal's office, where the dog gratefully ate the remains of Benteen's supper, and then came and sat at his feet.

'It's going to be a long night, dog,' he said. 'I'm sure glad of the company.' The dog barked. 'Now, I can't keep calling you dog, can I? I've got to give you a name. I'll have to think about what that name might be.'

He had by now decided that the town doctor had not broken his confidence. And that Henry Blue being a member of the Freedom Brotherwood was as crazy an idea as he'd ever had.

'Us!' the assembled members of the Jewel Creek Chapter of the Freedom Brotherhood cried out in unison, at the Chapter Leader's suggestion that they raid the marshal's office and retrieve the gold.

'Who else?' the Chapter Leader growled. 'We can't hire help, can we? Who's going to believe that we'd go to the trouble of waylaying, maybe even killing Benteen, to get our hands on a crate of farm implements?'

'But we're no thugs,' the man called Sidney moaned.

'Killing the marshal?' a second man questioned, shaking his head vehemently in rejection of the idea.

'If there's no other way that we can retrieve the gold, yes,' the Chapter Leader confirmed. He looked with contempt at the quaking men. 'You didn't expect to start a revolution and not get blood on your hands, did you?'

'Benteen is rawhide tough,' the third man cautioned. 'And by his utterances, wouldn't give the Freedom Brotherhood any quarter.'

'And that's a real shame,' the Chapter Leader said, his regret obvious. 'The revolution will need men of the marshal's grit, if it's to succeed.'

'There isn't any question of it not succeeding, is there?' the fourth man asked the Chapter Leader, his pallor evidence of the leap his mind had made to the consequences for those who had been party to the treachery of the Freedom Brotherhood, should the revolt fizzle out.

'Any revolution has its elements of doubt and luck,' the Chapter Leader said unsympathetically, and then reckoned, on seeing the glum faces of the other men, that he had better strike a note of optimism before they took off like scared rabbits. 'But with the backing of the Mexicans, there's no way we can fail. By the time the forces of the US can respond, the revolution will be unstoppable. And,' he looked proudly from man to man, 'we'll go down in history as being the men who saved America from those who would destroy it. Because, gentlemen, I haven't told you before now: when the men hiding out in the hills between here and Hadley Wells rise up, it will be the signal to the hundreds of Chapters throughout America to join us.'

The rallying speech renewed the men's flagging spirits and boosted their confidence. The Chapter Leader's relief was immense. The responsibility on his Chapter, and his leadership, to start the revolution was both a great honour and an awesome burden. He would have wished for men with the kind of backbone that Seth Benteen had; men who, once committed, would fight to the bitter end, even in the face of certain defeat, and maybe plant the seeds for a later uprising by their heroism.

'Maybe one of us could ride into the hills and get help.'

The Chapter Leader looked with undisguised contempt at the speaker. 'Wouldn't that look just great,' he glowered. 'First sign of trouble and we turn tail! Now what would that do for morale?' The men lowered their eyes under his furious glare. 'Getting that gold is our problem. Anyway, we haven't got time to get help.'

'So when do we act?' a member asked.

'Right now.'

'Tonight?' Sidney yelped.

'We haven't got time to spare,' the Chapter Leader said. 'What do you think will happen if this down on its luck town finds out that there's a quarter of a million dollars there for the taking?'

'How're we going to get into the marshal's office, without him shooting us full of holes?' was the next question asked of the Chapter Leader.

'Sidney,' he said, addressing the dapper, slight of frame gent, 'you're going to get Benteen to come out.'

'I am?' Sidney asked, puzzled. 'How do I do that?'

CHAPTER EIGHT

Thirty minutes later, huddled in the darkness of an alley across the street from the marshal's office, the Chapter Leader's plan was clear. The man called Sidney was dressed as a woman, and looking every inch the part, right down to the blonde wig, hair the same colour as the woman he reckoned would have the Jewel Creek marshal running from his office to her aid.

'You and you,' the Chapter Leader ordered two of the men, 'take up positions in the alley alongside the marshal's office, and in the door of the dressmaker's shop next door. I'll hide behind the water trough outside. You remain here,' he instructed the fourth man of the Freedom Brotherhood Chapter. 'You're the straightest shooter. I don't imagine that we'll fail to immobilize the marshal. But if we do, you shoot him.'

'Shooting at one o'clock in the morning will

have the dead rising up,' Sidney pointed out, his voice quaking.

'If we're quick, the gold can be grabbed and loaded onto the wagon.' A sympathizer with their cause, the town livery owner Ned Blake, had made a wagon ready and it was waiting at the end of the alley across from the marshal's office to haul the gold out of town. 'Ned Blake knows this country better than most men. He'll be able to make the wagon vanish in no time at all. It'll be in the hills to pay for those guns, pronto.'

Sidney's eyes flashed round the other men, who shared his doubt.

'Ned Blake's got a chequered history,' a man called Ed said. 'Can we trust him to deliver the gold?'

'A lot of men who'll fight in this revolution will have a chequered history,' the Chapter Leader pointed out. 'Mercenary armies aren't top drawer gents. In fact, lining their pockets from the chaos of conflict is their main reason for fighting in the first place. After the revolt, in calmer times, the riff-raff can be weeded out and dealt with.'

'So what if Ned Blake takes off with the gold?' Ed pressed the Chapter Leader.

'You've got to admit that it's a hell of a treasure,' another member of the Chapter said.

'And a mighty temptation,' another added. 'I figure that someone should go with Blake.'

'No one can be missing from town. Might as well

put up a shingle over your door announcing that you heisted the gold. You have my guarantee that Blake will deliver the gold.'

'How can you be so sure,' Sidney questioned.

The Chapter Leader took from his pocket an envelope and held it up. 'Because in this letter, I've told him that if he gets greedy, his entire family will be killed.' The Chapter members exchanged shocked glances. 'I'll tell him to read it once he's clear of town. He'll think that it contains some extra instructions.' He smiled evilly. 'His house is being watched.'

'But that's—'

'Cold-blooded murder?' the Chapter Leader put to the man who had spoken. His shrug was one of indifference. 'Can't make an omlette without breaking eggs. Folk, lots of folk, get killed in an uprising. Better get used to sleeping with ghosts haunting you, gents.'

The man who had previously suggested they seek help from the revolutionaries in the hills, again put forward that it would be best to have a band of them ride in and take the gold by force. 'It will leave us out of the picture, if anything goes wrong.'

This got the whole-hearted support of his compatriots.

'I've told you,' the Chapter Leader growled. 'We haven't got time! Benteen will be shipping the gold out on the noon train.'

66

'How do you know that?' Ed asked.

The Chapter Leader ignored his question.

'The earliest one of us could make it back from the hills with the men would be late tomorrow. The gold would be long gone by then.'

'Shipping it out to where?' Ed asked.

'The governor's office.'

'Damn!' Sidney swore.

The Chapter Leader grinned. 'That ain't no language for a pretty lady,' he said, ruffling Sidney's blonde wig.

The brief, humourous interlude relieved the men's gloom, but only momentarily.

'If the gold is on the train, we could rob it,' was Ed's next suggestion to the Chapter Leader.

'We're no train robbers,' the Chapter Leader said testily, tired of objections and obstacles. 'And train guards shoot back.' He went on resolutely, 'The gold has to be snatched now. It's the middle of the night, and there's only the marshal standing between us and that crate he's got stashed in the jail.' He glared at his partners in the Freedom Brotherhood.

'Now let's get it done!' he ordered. He shoved Sidney across the street. 'The rest of you take up your positions. You've got the most important role,' he told Sidney. 'Play your part right, and Seth Benteen will be out of that office quicker than a fox's jaws clamping on a hen.'

*

67

Marshal Seth Benteen was woken from the doze he had slipped into by the mongrel's low growl. He came instantly alert, cursing his slide into slumber.

'What is it? What're you hearing, dog?'

He strained, but could not hear a thing. However, trusting the dog's instincts, the marshal reached behind to the gunrack for a rifle. The mongrel got up and went to the door, ears cocked, his gaze intent. Taking his cue from the dog, Benteen joined him. His problem was that if he looked out with the lamp still burning, he'd not see a thing. And, as previously, if he lowered or quenched the lamp, whoever was outside would know that he had been alerted to their presence. All he could practically do was listen and be ready, should trouble come a-calling. Tense seconds passed before he heard footsteps on the boardwalk outside, by their lightness, a woman's footsteps he judged. But what woman would be out and about in the small hours of the morning? Then heavier and quicker moving footsteps. The sounds of a struggle had Benteen opening the law-office door marginally. He poked the barrel of the rifle out the couple of inches of space. He forced the growling mongrel back until the situation became clearer. Suddenly a woman, her face averted from the narrow beam of light from the office lamp, lurched forward and toppled in to the street directly outside. Boots clipped it in the opposite direction. It was Lucy Brown. She'd been attacked!

Distraught, Seth Benteen ran to Lucy's aid. The Chapter Leader of the Freedom Brotherhood had accurately assessed Seth Benteen's reaction. He had barely left the safety of the marshal's office when he knew that he had been duped. Shadows on either side of him loomed up. And, on closer scrutiny, the woman he thought was Lucy Brown was a man, but he had craftily fallen to the ground with his back to the marshal to hide his identity.

The mongrel sprang from the office to Benteen's side, but a gunbutt floored the dog, as another did the same to the Jewel Creek marshal. Swirling into a deep pit of unconsciousness, Benteen knew that whoever had organized the raid on the jail, knew him very well indeed, and had perfectly judged his response to the distress the woman he was in love with would bring.

Sinking into a black hole, the fact that he was in love with Lucy Brown held no surprise for him. At least, he thought wryly, the gunbutt that had knocked him senseless had, on the other hand, knocked sense into him.

CHAPTER NINE

When he came to, Benteen's immediate concern was for the mongrel. The dog was still stretched out on the boardwalk where he had been callously cut down. Probably dead, was the marshal's first gloomy thought, an emotion that quicky turned to rage. He dragged himself to where the dog was lying and shook him. The lawman's relief was great when the dog moaned and his pain-filled eyes rolled upwards.

Benteen grinned.

'I know the feeling, partner,' he croaked.

If asked, Seth Benteen could not give an answer as to who helped who into the law office. The Jewel Creek lawman made his way to the jail behind the office, knowing well what he would find, an empty cell where the crate of gold had been. As his head cleared, his anger rose in direct proportion. And mixed in with his anger was a sense of sad disappointment that he had been betrayed by a man he had trusted – Henry Blue. There was no other way to reason what had happened. The Jewel Creek doctor was the only one he had confided in, and therefore he could be the only one who had passed on the secret he had shared with him. But to whom in town had he passed it on? Or had he passed it on at all? Perhaps the town doctor had gone and rounded up a couple of his friends or a bevy of the town dregs and had raided the jail himself. Either to enrich himself, or in some misguided attempt to improve the lot of the townsfolk who had fallen on hard times. Benteen's mind went back to re-run Blue's ponderings on what the gold would do for the town. But whatever the reason for the robbery of the gold, the plain fact was that it was still a robbery and the law had been broken, not to mention the lump on his and the mongrel's skulls.

'Dog,' he said grimly, 'I reckon it's time to pay a visit to the good Doc Blue.'

'Take these swishes,' the Jewel Creek Chapter Leader of the Freedom Brotherhood, instructed his cohorts, 'and wipe out the wagon tracks.'

The Chapter members, elated by their success, gladly obliged. Their dreams now were of a new order: an order that would unashamedly favour its supporters. And like Ned Blake, and the men whose characters and motives they had questioned, they too hoped to enrich themselves. In

71

fact, had one of them the courage to propose that they should keep the gold for themselves, it might very well have happened that way, over the Chapter Leader's dead body, of course.

The Chapter Leader was a man who wanted nothing in the way of financial reward from the coming revolution. His belief in a new order sprang from outright conviction, rather than grabbing any opportunity for self-advancement. After the revolution, he'd be a really dangerous man, from the point of view of those less dedicated to the doctrine the Freedom Brotherhood espoused. And like all true revolutionaries would probably be quickly disposed of by the more pragmatic among them.

'That should do it,' the Chapter Leader told the zealously brushing Chapter members, when they reached the outskirts of town. 'There'll be a thousand and one wagon tracks from here on from the normal traffic of commerce. You head off home, gents.' His eyes shone with the fire of fanaticism. 'The next time we'll get together will be to come out in public to hail and toast the revolution.'

The Chapter members hurried away into the night. When the Chapter Leader reached home, he went quietly to the den at the rear of the house. From the safe he took the detailed progress chart of the revolution. First, would come the attack on the army fort south of Hadley Wells. Taken, that would allow the Mexican troops unhindered progress across the Rio Grande, to join up with the revolutionary forces at the fort for the march on the territorial capital.

The Chapter Leader regretted that American would kill American. However, that had happened already. This time America would emerge from the bloodshed, guided by the ethos of the Freedom Brotherhood.

Marshal Seth Benteen cautiously approached Henry Blue's house. The house was in darkness, suggesting that Henry was either fast asleep, or out and about hiding or conveying gold. Of course there was one other possibility, and that was that as a result of his treachery, the Jewel Creek doctor might be waiting in the dark house for Benteen's inevitable visit. Blue had little familiarity with weapons, so he would not be a great shot. That meant that his choice of weapon would be something else, like a knife or a blunt instrument to crack open a skull that had already been dented.

The Jewel Creek marshal observed the house from behind a stout oak, his eyes patiently wandering over the house for the slightest sign of Henry Blue's presence. There was none. Maybe he had lit out with his partners in crime, if crime it was from the doctor's point of view. A deeply compassionate man, Henry Blue worried about the poverty which had beset the town after the mine's closure, and in fact gave of his services free to those who could not pay. However, Seth Benteen's jaw set grimly, as far as the law was concerned a robbery had been perpetrated and Henry Blue was the prime suspect in that robbery either by self-deed or by complicity with others to whom he had passed information about the treasure in the Jewel Creek jail.

Thankfully, the night was cloudy, and the marshal (crouched to make himself a smaller target in case a more gun-handy friend of Henry Blue's had him in his sights) could move reasonably freely across the yard to the house. He pressed against the side of the house, near the kitchen window, listening for any tell-tale sign of where trouble might spring from. Hearing nothing, after a couple of minutes, he tried the kitchen window and found it latched. He moved on along the wall to where he knew the parlour window was and tried it – it too was locked. Henry Blue was a security conscious man. After another five minutes of searching, he stumbled on the cellar doors and, fortunately, found them open. Entering the celler, he was hoping that the door at the top of the cellar stairs leading into the house would be unlocked. It was. Benteen eased the cellar door open on regularly oiled hinges, and stepped into the dark hallway, up from which ran a wide staircase.

Again, he paused and listened.

A wind had sprung up and mournfully sighed through the house, like a bevy of ghosts whispering to each other. Being a man of direct action, stealth unnerved Seth Benteen. The eerie stillness of the house crept into him, filling him with a sense of foreboding.

He looked along the panelled hall with its many doors, any one of which might spring open to reveal a surprise he'd not welcome. But searched the house would have to be.

Tensed, standing to the left of the door, sixgun cocked, Seth Benteen opened the first door.

CHAPTER TEN

The door to Henry Blue's library (his favourite room in the house, and the one where he spent most of his spare time, the little of which he had, being the only doctor between Jewel Creek and Hadley Wells) swung open. The marshal winced as its hinges creaked, not loudly, but in the still of the night too loudly. The dying embers of a log fire collapsed in the grate and sent a shower of sparks racing up the chimney. A sudden shaft of orange and blue flame sent ghostly shadows dancing round the room and reflected off the polished spines of books lining the library walls from floor to ceiling. By now, Benteen could see most of the library and there was no sign of the doctor. But knowing the geography of the room from his many social visits to the house, he knew that there was a nook to the right of the door which he still could not see and, of course, Henry Blue could be waiting behind the door to crack his skull open.

The Jewel Creek lawman edged into the room, inch by cautious inch.

Ned Blake, the livery owner was relieved to see the back of Jewel Creek, and eased back on the team hauling the heavy wagon. He turned in the seat to look back at the crate sitting dead centre of the wagon, and could still not quite believe that inside the innocent looking box marked Farm Implements, there was a quarter of a million dollars in gold.

'Heck,' he murmured breathlessly, licking parched lips. 'What a man could do with a quarter of a million dollars.' Then he became even more breathless. 'And a hundred times more in Mexico. What if I turned this little ol' wagon south, and just kept goin' 'cross the Rio Grande,' he murmured.

However, he resisted the urge to do that, and kept the wagon on a trail leading into the hills. Not because he was a zealot for the cause. The coming revolution was an event that he hoped would help him out of the debt he had been plunged into when Jewel Creek had suddenly folded as a viable town, and he needed a stake to quit the no-hope burg. No, his true reason for his enforced honesty was that, should he abscond with the gold, he would also be leaving behind his wife and three kids, all of whom he loved dearly. And he doubted very much if a quarter of a million dollars could buy him the happiness he had with his family.

He shifted in the seat and brushed against the letter the Chapter Leader had given him before he'd left town.

'Read this letter when you're a couple of miles out of town,' had been the Chapter Leader's orders. 'And read it very carefully, Ned,' he added sombrely.

Well, he reckoned that at about three miles from Jewel Creek, it was about time to read the letter.

'Henry,' Benteen said. 'You there?'

Heck, would he answer if he was, if doing him mischief was what the doc had in mind. In a sudden, swift movement, Seth Benteen threw himself behind a sofa from where he could see into the nook at the far end of the room, the only place where Henry Blue could now be hiding. There was no one in the room. And that meant that he would have to live on his nerves for a spell longer while he checked out the other rooms along the hall, and maybe upstairs too. Ten minutes later, he arrived at the Jewel Creek doctor's bedroom. As with every other room, he eased open the door.

Ned Blake had been curious about the contents of the letter the Chapter Leader had given him. It could not contain instructions as to how he would reach his destination, because that he knew. Over the past month he had done at least six dry runs, so that when the time came to make the real run, he'd be able to do it blindfolded.

The Jewel Creek livery owner saw no need to pull off the trail to strike a match to read the letter, but the Chapter Leader had drilled in to him the need to continuously take precautions. 'Even when there seems to be no need, Ned,' he'd repeatedly stressed. So now he parked the wagon in a small stand of trees off the trail, before he opened the letter and read its contents. As he did so, his jaw dropped, and then a terrible fear took him over, because he recognized the genuineness of the terrible threat the letter held. It read:

Dear Ned,
In case you're tempted to head for Mexico with the Chapter's gold, before you do, know that someone is watching your house. And if the gold doesn't arrive where it should, that someone is under strict orders to slaughter your entire family.

So weak was Ned Blake, that he thought that he could not go on, but he knew that he had to. Not for a second did he doubt the Chapter Leader's resolve to carry out the awful revenge on his family if he failed in his mission.

As the door to Henry Blue's bedroom swung open, Marshal Seth Benteen was gripped by the most awful fear. And before the door had opened fully, he knew by instinct that the Jewel Creek doctor was dead. Death had a presence, and the room was rife with it.

Henry Blue lay across the bed in his nightshirt. The bed was awash with blood from the deep slash in the doctor's throat, so deep in fact was it, that Henry Blue's head hung on a tendril of gristle. Benteen gagged at the sight. The West was a lawless place, and murder was not uncommon. But a murder of such gruesome brutality, even in the raw West, was an abomination. For Benteen, if there was even a modicum of consolation to be found, it was in knowing that Henry Blue had not been a party to the raid on the jail. And that he had obviously not willingly broken the bond of trust with him. But obviously having suffered terrible agony, Henry had been forced to reveal the secret of Jewel Creek to his murderer.

'Now who could that evil bastard be?' the marshal murmured.

CHAPTER ELEVEN

Seth Benteen was floundering. He was a good town marshal but no ace detective. His talent was for knocking heads together in the saloon and tossing drunks in jail. He was handy with a gun, but that talent would in no way help him to find the doctor's killer. Where to begin to unravel the mystery of Henry Blue's murder evaded him. He knew there were several men involved in the heisting of the gold, but he had not seen any of them clearly. Pacing Henry Blue's bedroom, searching for a direction in which to go, the Jewel Creek marshal suddenly stopped in his tracks. One of the thieves had dressed to look like Lucy Brown to lure him outside. So that meant that the brains behind the heist knew exactly what his reaction to Lucy's distress would be. Now how many men in town had that knowledge, and were that clever? Art Brown came to mind. Although he had never said, Brown would know from his reaction whenever his niece

81

put in an appearance when he had worked in the Brown grainstore and later when he became marshal and was invited on the odd occasion to dinner at the house, that his feelings for Lucy ran deep. And Brown also qualified when it came to cleverness. But Art Brown a murderer and a thief? Ridiculous, was Seth Benteen's conclusion. The Jewel Creek store-owner was one of the most upright and honest men he had ever encountered.

'So, now that you've ruled out Art Brown,' Benteen sighed, 'who's left?'

The marshal did a quick mental check on who else might fit the picture, and drew a blank. The brutality of Henry Blue's murder would indicate a rougher element in town. Saloon dregs, who'd slit their own mother's throat for a nickel. Maybe it had started out as a simple robbery, and somehow the killer or killers had struck a rich vein of good luck and had somehow learned of the gold in the jail. Perhaps Henry had tried to trade knowledge for life?

'Or maybe one of them saw me haul the crate into the jail and took to wondering about what was in it,' Benteen speculated. He had addressed Henry Blue's lifeless form. 'And then when they saw you leave after your visit, Henry, and knowing how often we gabbed, followed you home? Figuring that you might know what was in the crate.

'I'll do my darnest to nail the bastard who did

this to you, Henry,' he promised.

But would saloon dregs have the brain to organize the heist of the gold in such a clever fashion? Now Benteen's thoughts took another turn. Henry was in his bedroom. And since his wife had passed away, being a man of strong appetites, he had sought the company of a particular saloon dove who secretly visited his house late at night – at least Henry thought her visits were a secret. Had Mamie Long shared Henry's bed tonight? Some of the world's greatest secrets had been revealed between the sheets. History attested to that fact. Mamie Long was as rotten as they come, but clever too. For Henry's benefit, she was always the lady. But Benteen had heard with his own ears how she mocked Henry in the saloon. If Henry had told Mamie about the gold, then that would lead back directly to the saloon and the dregs of the town.

'Goddamit, Henry!' Benteen growled. 'You've posed me one hell of a problem. My head is reeling, dammit!'

Controlling his anger, he headed for the door.

'Better get Mort Hanson to the house,' he said. 'And get you to the funeral parlour. Then, I guess I'll start my investigations at the saloon.' At the door he turned back and sniffed at the bed clothes. 'No perfume,' he muttered. 'Like the kind a lady would leave behind.' But then, he recalled that Henry Blue reacted badly to perfumes, and fancy scented soap made his eyes water. Therefore, maybe Mamie Long had washed off the scent she wore in the saloon before visiting Henry. Bedrooms were not places where guests, other than the Mamie Long variety, were entertained.

Seth Benteen's brow furrowed on his next thought springing to mind. Henry Blue sometimes got fainting spells. He had given him a key to the house to check on him, if he did not show in town at his office when he was supposed to on the dot of 9.15 every morning. And, troublingly, there was one other man in town to whom Henry had entrusted a key. . . .

Art Brown.

CHAPTER TWELVE

The Silver Slipper saloon was the kind of estab-
lishment that never closed. Sam Brennan, the
owner was a bachelor and a chronic insomniac,
and the combination of loneliness and sleepless-
ness saw him spend most of his time behind the
bar. And when he did sleep for a brief period, he
lay down on a couch in a parlour off the bar. At
1.30 a.m. there wasn't much business. And when
Seth Benteen stepped through the batwings,
Brennan gave up on the drunk who was rambling
on and making no sense, and came to serve the
marshal, surprised by Benteen's visit. Brennan
knew of the Jewel Creek marshal's past fondness
for liquor, and the only time he visited the saloon
was to knock heads together when rowdiness
broke out. Of late, with the town's slide into
depression, his visits had been frequent. But a visit
in the small hours of the morning could not be
business, Brennan reckoned. And he wondered if

he should pour for Benteen or not. Brennan admired the marshal's climb back from the gutter. But he need not have worried.

'Mamie Long entertaining, Sam?' the marshal enquired. 'Wouldn't want to bust in on any fun and games.'

Sam Brennan shook his head.

'Monday night. Business is slow.' He sighed. 'Business is slow every night now, Seth.'

Benteen nodded towards the stairs. 'OK if I go up?'

'Mamie can be pretty short-tempered when disturbed,' Brennan cautioned. 'Except when it's business.'

'It's business sure enough,' Benteen said, crossing the bar to the stairs. 'But not the kind of business you've got in mind, Sam.'

'I guess you're saving it all for Lucy Brown, eh, Seth?'

Why did everyone in Jewel Creek figure that Lucy Brown had a hankering for him? Or maybe he was reading that wrong. Maybe it was his hankering for her that everyone was talking about.

The drunk sprang off his chair, gave a loud howl, and crashed on to the floor. Benteen went to pick the man up.

'Don't bother,' was Brennan's advice. 'He'll sleep perfectly peaceful right where he is.'

Benteen went upstairs. As a precaution, on reaching Mamie Long's door, he put his ear to it to listen for any sounds that would indicate that Mamie was entertaining. He knew that sometimes Mamie's visitors came to her room through the window at the end of the hall from the outside stairs. That way she did not have to hand over half of what she got to Brennan. Hearing nothing but the sigh of the easterly wind curling round the side of the building, he knocked on the door, gently at first and then more vigorously when he got no response.

'Go 'way!' came the saloon dove's spiky response. 'A girl needs her rest, you know.'

'It ain't business. It's Marshal Benteen. Open the door, Mamie,' he commanded.

After a load of shuffling and no small amount of swearing, the door opened and Mamie Long's tussled brown head poked out.

'Did you visit Henry Blue tonight?' he asked bluntly.

'Henry Blue,' she snorted. 'The doc ain't a man who—'

'Did you?' the marshal interjected impatiently.

'No,' the dove said sourly. 'Haven't visited Henry in an age. I reckon he's gone right off me, Marshal.' She became bitter. 'Getting too long in the tooth, I figure. Utah Lil's disappeared a couple of times recently though. Barely out of nappies, that gal.'

'What's her room number?'

'Six.'

'Sorry for disturbing your sleep,' Benteen apologized.

'Now that you have, Marshal . . .' Mamie Long leant forward to tempt Benteen with a show of cleavage. When he showed no interest, she said bitterly, 'Maybe if I was a goody two shoes like Lucy Brown.'

The room door slammed.

'Damn,' Benteen swore. 'There ain't nothing going on between me and Lucy Brown! Can't the folk in this town get that through their heads!'

He stormed back along the hall to hammer on the door of room six.

'Whoever you are, go away,' came back the brusque reply to his summons.

'Utah,' the Jewel Creek lawman called out, 'This is Seth Benteen, and I aim to talk to you right now, gal. So you're either coming out, or I'm coming in. What's it to be?'

A moment later the room door opened an inch.

'What's all the hullabaloo about,' Utah Lil groused. 'Can't lawmen read time?'

No one knew Utah Lil by any other name. Benteen had been at the train depot the day, almost a year ago, when she had arrived in town and Sam Brennan had come to meet her, signalling her profession.

'What's your name, honey?' a wag had asked. 'Got to call you somethin' when I'm whisperin' to ya on your pillow.'

'Utah Lil,' she had replied.

'That ain't a name,' the man had said.

'It's the only one you or anyone else around here is going to get, mister,' Utah Lil had replied feistily. 'And you and everyone else can take it or leave it.'

That day Seth Benteen felt sorry for Utah Lil, because she was not the usual run of saloon woman. There was something about her that said that she should never have to see the inside of a saloon, let alone in the capacity she was then entering one.

Sam Brennan had ushered her away to his buggy. Later, Benteen had dropped by to let his views be known on the unsuitability of Utah Lil for doving.

'She's a grown woman, Marshal,' had been Brennan's response. 'I ain't forcing her to stay put.'

'That's right, Marshal.'

Benteen had swung around to face Utah Lil, already in costume and ready to engage in her trade.

Benteen had tipped his hat. 'Ma'am.' She was right. What she chose to do or not do, provided it did not break the law in a serious way, was her own business, and he'd left. A couple of weeks later he had heard from a fella passing through town that Utah Lil's real name was Katherine Ford, and she had been a schoolteacher back in Utah.

'Guess she likes what she does,' was the stranger's reply to Benteen, when he had pondered on why a schoolteacher would be selling herself in a saloon.

'Well?' Utah Lil snapped. 'What do you want, Marshal?'

'If you've got someone in there, I think it would be best to step in to the hall,' the marshal suggested.

Utah Lil glanced back into the room, and then stepped into the hall.

'I hear that Henry Blue's taken a liking to you, Utah. That right?'

'And if it is?'

'Did you see Henry tonight?' Benteen questioned.

'And if I did?'

'Don't sass me!' the Jewel Creek lawman growled. 'Just answer the damn question.'

'No. I did not. Is that answer enough.'

'Sure?'

'I'm sure. 'Night, Marshal.'

Utah Lil squeezed back through the door, careful to curtail a view of the room to Benteen. Not that he wanted to see who Utah Lil's customer was – a man had a right to his privacy. But when the dove's nightdress caught on the edge of the door, for a moment before she grabbed at it, he saw something that surprised him no end. In a wardrobe mirror he caught a glimpse of a man sprawled naked on the bed, and that man was Art Brown. Of all the men in Jewel Creek, Art was the last man he'd have expected to use the services of a saloon woman. But then when he thought about it, he decided that even men on pedestals got their urges. However, reason it out as he might, for Seth Benteen, the store-keeper had lost some of his saintly glow. And he was not sure yet whether he was pleased that Art was like other mortals. Or disappointed that the store-owner had feet of clay. But either way, what Art got up to was none of his business.

The room door slammed shut.

Ned Blake was rocked to his very core by the contents of the letter that the Chapter Leader had given him, and his first reaction was to turn the wagon and head back to town to seek Seth Benteen's help. He had the names of the other Chapter members he could trade with, but he was hauling a wagonload of gold stolen from the marshal and, instead of listening, the Jewel Creek lawman might just sling him in jail and throw away the key.

Blake did not for a second doubt the threat in the letter. The stakes were much too high for the Chapter Leader of the Freedom Brotherhood to be bluffing. And word of his return would get out in no time at all. In fact, a wagon rolling into town at dead of night would attract immediate attention. So even if the marshal believed him, Sarah and the kids would be dead before they ever got near his house, which was about a mile out of town. The Chapter Leader was a shrewd and clever man, and he probably had staked out the trail for any sign of him wavering. Returning to town was a gamble he could not take. He had no choice but to go on. But he was no longer interested in the potential rewards that the revolution would bring him. His only thought now was for the revenge he would take on the Chapter Leader when next he met up with him.

Benteen was slumped in his chair in the marshal's office, at a loss as to where he should turn to next, now that the one lead he had followed had fizzled out. He had spent the best part of two hours trying to figure out who had murdered Henry Blue, and his head ached from not having come up with a solitary suspect. The fact that Art Brown had a key to Henry Blue's house should make the store-keeper a prime suspect. However, though he had just seen a side of the store-keeper he had not suspected, there was a wide gulf between a man indulging his appetites and murder.

He shifted uneasily at the prospect of having to question Art Brown.

The mongrel looked up at him.

'I know, dog,' he growled. 'I'm the law and it's my clear duty.'

The mongrel barked.

'You're sure a big help!' He checked the time on the wall clock. Almost an hour since he'd seen the store owner in Utah Lil's company. 'I figure that Art should be back in his own bed by now, don't you?'

The mongrel barked again.

'OK, I'm on my way, you pesky mongrel.'

As he made his way to the Brown house at the end of the main street, Seth Benteen wondered which door the gold might be hidden? And what door did the thieves hide behind? Or maybe the gold had already left town? After talking to Art Brown, he'd take a lamp and search for wagon tracks.

'That's something you should have done in the first place,' he rebuked himself. 'You're not the world's best detective, are you, Benteen?'

He used the fine brass knocker on Art Brown's door to announce his arrival.

CHAPTER THIRTEEN

'What do *you* want?' Lucy Brown asked sharply on opening the front door.

'I need to talk to Art, Lucy,' Benteen said, disappointed at the hostility shown him.

'It's the small hours of the morning. My uncle's been in bed for hours.'

That was true. But not in his own bed.

'It's important, Lucy.'

'That will be Miss Brown to you, Marshal.'

'Yes, ma'am,' Benteen said, his heart stung by Lucy's rebuke. 'But I still need to talk to your uncle.' His features set in stone. 'In fact, I insist.'

Lucy Brown was taken aback. 'Insist, did you say, Marshal Benteen?'

'Insist, ma'am,' the Jewel Creek lawman unequivocally stated.

'What seems to be the trouble, Lucy?' The man who had come from a room along the hall which

Seth knew to be the den, had a book in his hand and a curious look on his face. He held up the book he was carrying. 'I wasn't sleeping very well, so I came down to read.'

The man looked questioningly beyond Lucy to Benteen.

'The marshal is,' she scoffed, '*insisting* on seeing my Uncle, Charles.' So this was Charles Barrington, Lucy's beau and intended husband, if Art Brown was on the right track. 'Did you ever hear such impudent nonsense!'

'Don't fret so, darling.' Barrington came forward quickly to comfort Lucy, putting an arm around her waist and drawing her possessively to him. 'Now, Marshal,' he began pompously, 'I'm sure that whatever your business with Art is, it can wait until a more civilized time to be conducted. Goodnight, sir.'

The front door was closing when Seth Benteen shoved it open again.

'Look here, Marshal,' Barrington protested. 'Your behaviour is out of order and upsetting to Lucy.'

'I'm not moving an inch until I see Art. Understood?' the marshal growled.

'Oh, Charles, do be careful,' Lucy said fretfully, on seeing the grim set of Seth Benteen's jaw.

'Leave this to me, Lucy.'

He tried to shove Benteen out the door.

'Don't do that, fella,' the lawman said, in the

quiet way he spoke when his anger was reaching a peak.

'Oh. And why not?'

Barrington shoved again. Seth Benteen's right fist shot out and landed squarely on Barrington's jaw, spinning him backwards into the hall and onto his backside, bemused. Lucy rushed to comfort him.

'Are you all right, darling?' she asked, concerned.

'Don't mollycoddle him,' Seth Benteen barked. 'It's his own damn fault. He should have known better than to manhandle.'

'I swear, if you don't leave right now, I'll get my uncle's gun and . . . and . . .'

Art Brown appeared at the top of the stairs.

'What the devil's gotten into everyone?' he enquired. 'Seth, what're you doing here at this time?'

After his visit to Utah Lil, Seth Benteen reckoned that that was a question which the Jewel Creek store-keeper had no need to ask.

'Could we talk in private, Art?' Benteen said.

'I don't see why not, Seth,' Brown said amiably.

'Uncle Art,' Lucy Brown whined. 'Mr Benteen has assaulted Charles. So there should be no place for him in this house, now or ever!'

'How did that come about?' Brown asked.

'Charles tried to eject the marshal to protect me,' Lucy said. 'And the marshal struck out. A fine way for a man who's sworn to uphold the law to be behaving, I say. You are a disgrace to your badge, Marshal,' she fumed.

'Now settle down everyone.' Art Brown came downstairs. 'I'm sure that all of this was just a misunderstanding.' He led the way along the hall to the den. 'Let's talk, Seth.'

As Benteen passed Lucy, she threw him a furious look of hot hatred. Barrington also glared at him, but the fury in him was of the stone-cold variety, the deadliest anger of all. The marshal had no doubt that in Charles Barrington he had made an enemy as dangerous as a trod on rattler, and he wondered how Lucy Brown could be attracted to the man. He had smooth looks and well-groomed hair, his hands were soft and his nails were clean. But there was something about him that indicated rottenness inside. How could Lucy not see it? But she was afflicted by the blindness of love. Or, maybe, Benteen thought, embittered by disappointment and no small amount of jealousy, he was seeing in Barrington the image of a man he wanted to see?

Art Brown closed the den door and went to sit behind the desk. He sat for a spell, looking steadily at Benteen, before he spoke.

'You saw, didn't you, Seth? When Utah Lil's nightdress snagged on the door and jerked it open.'

'Ain't none of my business, Art.'

'You'll keep my secret, Seth?' he asked, heavy-shouldered.

'I'll keep it,' the lawman promised.

'I don't visit very often. Only when—'

'There's no need to explain, Art. A man's got his needs.' He sighed heavily. 'Henry Blue's been murdered.'

The store-owner sat perfectly still. It was not the reaction Benteen had expected from Brown on hearing such tragic news about a friend. But men reacted in different ways to such tidings.

'You've got a key to Henry's house, Art. . . .'

'So have you, Seth. So what are you saying?'

'I've got to ask you if you've been round to Henry's house tonight?'

'You think I might have murdered Henry?'

'No.'

'Then why all the ruckus at dead of night?'

'Only doing my job, Art. A man's been murdered. With a killer on the loose, the sooner questions that need asking are asked, all the better.'

'No, I wasn't anywhere near Henry Blue's house tonight, Seth.' He stood up. 'Is that all?'

'I guess.' There was one other question he needed to ask, but he was at the den door when he got up the grit to ask it. 'Where's your key to Henry's house, Art?'

'Why?'

'You've still got it, haven't you?'

'Sure.' He opened the desk drawer. 'It's

right. . . .' He rooted through the drawer's contents. 'Was right here,' he concluded, puzzled.

'When did you see the key last, Art?'

'Yesterday, I think.'

He tried the other drawers of the desk, without success. 'Can't fathom it out. Who'd want to steal the key of Henry Blue's house, Seth?'

'His killer, Art,' the Jewel Creek marshal said.

Had the key really been stolen? Or was Art Brown trying to send him on a wild goose chase to divert attention away from himself?

CHAPTER FOURTEEN

Before leaving, Benteen questioned Art Brown closely about the comings and goings to the house, and as the store-keeper answered, the marshal's heart sank more and more.

'Heck, Art,' Benteen groaned, as the list of possible thieves and murderers grew. 'It seems to me that most anyone in town could have stolen the key.'

'I don't believe in locked doors, Seth. You know that.'

He did. In his time working in Brown's grain-store, Benteen had free run of the house on errands. Owning several other businesses in town, the workers in those businesses also came and went. And there were Art's charitable works (providing a hot meal for those on hard times was one), when folk freely came and went. And the

store-keeper had a long list of friends and acquain-
tances, any of whom could drop by the house
unannounced. By the time the list was completed,
Seth Benteen was facing the gloomy prospect of
having most every man in town as Henry Blue's
possible killer. Where to turn to next, that was Seth
Benteen's problem. He was no Pinkerton detective, and all this detecting was putting him in a
spin.

'Are you all right, Uncle Art?' Lucy Brown
enquired, as she pushed past the marshal when he
opened the den door. She had obviously been waiting anxiously in the hall. She shot Benteen an
angry look. 'I hope you haven't upset Uncle Art,'
she snapped. 'I told him that you were trouble
when you arrived in town, and my mind hasn't
changed any since then, Seth Benteen.'

'Easy, girl,' her uncle counselled. 'Seth is only
doing his job.'

'Making a nuisance of himself, I'd say,' Lucy
flung back.

'You know, ma'am, you need a lot more honey
and a lot less gall,' Benteen said, riled by Lucy
Brown's ever present hostility toward him. The
marshal strode away, but paused before he left the
house. 'Didn't you ever hear of giving credit where
credit's due?'

Stunned by Seth Benteen's criticism, Lucy
Brown became thoughtful.

'Did you expect that Seth would forever hold his

tongue, Lucy?' Art Brown said, with a wry smile. 'And much as I hate to say so, he's got a point.'

'I guess he might have at that, Uncle Art,' she said, her mood reflective.

'The new America will need men of Benteen's strength of character and purpose.'

'The new America?' Lucy questioned her uncle.

Art Brown did not elaborate. 'You know,' the store-owner stood up and stretched, 'I think I'll take a stroll outside before going back to bed, Lucy.'

'Careful you don't catch a chill,' Lucy cautioned her uncle.

As Seth Benteen took long and angry strides to the marshal's office, had he paused for a moment to look behind him, he'd have seen Henry Blue's murderer watching him.

CHAPTER FIFTEEN

On reaching the law office, still smarting, Benteen took the lamp from the desk and left immediately, followed by the mongrel who had now taken up permanent residence with him. 'You got any ideas about this murder?' he said, as the mongrel looked at his friend. Benteen took to closely examining the ground near the jail first, and then continued to criss-cross the street looking for sign. 'They couldn't have lugged that gold away, unless, of course, the gold is stashed nearby and never left town. But I reckon the gold ain't in town. 'Cause the thieves prepared well for the heist. Planned every detail. So I figure that with that kind of planning, they had a wagon waiting, probably in this alley right here.'

Benteen entered the alley directly across from the jail. But his hope was soon dashed, when the dusty alley showed no sign of wagon wheels. Despondent, he leaned against the wall, defeated.

The mongrel came to sit alongside him, his tail swishing. Seth Benteen was looking at the dog's swishing tail scattering the dry dust of the alley for most of a minute before he sprang away from the wall, his eyes glowing with the insight that the mongrel's tail had given him, as to why there were no wagon wheel indentations. 'A swish, dog,' he enthused. He rubbed the dog's head. 'You're one cute critter, you know that,' he said, before resuming his examination of the alley and the backlot leading out of town, his pace quickening, certain that sooner or later he'd find what he was looking for. About a quarter of a mile outside of town, he found the indentation of the wagon wheels, and discarded alongside the track, a couple of willow swishes. He rubbed the mongrel's head. 'No Pinkerton would do as good as you have, dog. Heh, that's what I'll call you. Pinkerton.'

Seth Benteen's elation did not last for very long. He knew how the gold had been shifted. But he hadn't any idea where it had got to.

'Any other ideas in that head of yours, Pinkerton?' he asked the mongrel. 'I guess we've got a lot more thinking to do, huh. So let's head back to the law office and do just that. There's something that's niggling way inside my head. You got any ideas what that might be?'

Pinkerton barked.

'That's it, huh. Why didn't I think of that?'

He chuckled, and playfuly rubbed the mongrel's

head. The dog barked again. Almost too late, Seth Benteen realized that the mongrel was not being friendly, his bark was one of warning. The marshal dived behind an old rusted wagon, just a second before a rifle cracked and a bullet buzzed over his head. There followed the sound of running feet. Mad as a riled rattler, Benteen took off after the would-be assassin. Two more volleys had him diving for cover again. His task was futile, the bush-whacker was nimble of foot and had gained a lot of ground. Benteen cut along an alley that led to the main street, hoping to spot the shooter emerge further along from the backlot. But he was much too clever to make that mistake. Or there had been an open door for him to dart through. Alerted by the sound of gunfire, windows were opening and heads popping out.

'Go back to sleep,' Benteen called out. 'The excitement is over.'

Turning, he saw no sign of Pinkerton. He whistled, but the mongrel did not appear. Fearing that the the dog had caught a bullet, he quickly made his way back to where the shooting had started, but Pinkerton was nowhere to be found. He searched the backlot frantically, and further along he heard the dog whimpering. He struck a match, the lamp he had been carrying having been smashed when he had dived behind the wagon, and in its flare he saw Pinkerton stretched out on the ground, blood pouring from a gash on his head. He picked the dog up in his arms and hurried back to the jail to attend to the mongrel's wound. He was relieved to see that it was not as serious as it had at first seemed. It was more ugly than deadly. He bathed the wound and stopped the bleeding.

'You caught up with the critter, didn't you?' he said, settling the mongrel at his feet. Pinkerton looked up with mournful eyes and yawned, and it was only then that Benteen saw the traces of blood on the dog's teeth. 'You bit the bastard,' he said. 'And I sure hope you bit him good, Pinkerton.'

The following morning, the marshal strolled around town keeping a keen eye out for a man with a limp, and found him. And he was the last man he wanted to find.

CHAPTER SIXTEEN

'You shouldn't be standing on that leg, Uncle Art.' On hearing Lucy Brown's admonishment, Seth Benteen stopped dead in his tracks as he passed the general store. 'You should be at home resting. A wound like that could get real nasty. 'Don't you agree, Mrs Walters?' Lucy asked Alice Walters, who was trying to hide from Benteen the fancy round box that her wigs came in from back East as he stepped into the store. Alice had lost her hair a couple of years before during a bout of fever and it had never grown back. Under the blonde wigs she wore, she was completely bald. And it was the town's worst kept secret.

'Oh, fiddly, Lucy,' Brown groaned. 'Don't fuss so.'

'You!' Lucy Brown said scornfully, on seeing the marshal. 'It's all your damn fault that Uncle Art hurt himself in the first place.'

'It isn't befitting a young lady to swear, Lucy,' the

store-keeper rebuked his niece.

'I'm sorry, Uncle Art,' Lucy instantly apologized. 'It's just that I'd rather be in the company of a skunk than our marshal.'

'Hurt your leg, Art?' Benteen asked.

'Silliest thing. Last night, when you left, I couldn't settle to sleep. Went outside to get a breath of night air and caught my leg on the stump of an old tree. No need to fret, Seth. A day or two and I'll be fine.'

'Mind if I look, Art?'

'It's nothing, Seth.'

'With no doctor in town, if infection set in, you'd have to make your way to Hadley Wells. Best not wait if it's turning ugly. I've seen a lot of wounds in my time, so I reckon that I could tell, Art.'

'Like I said—'

'Show him your leg, Uncle,' Lucy commanded.

Reluctantly, the store-keeper pulled up the right leg of his trousers. There were purple patches on the wound, but no clear bite marks. However, the purple patches were in a line, which might point to the sinking of Pinkerton's teeth.

'Well?' Lucy questioned Benteen.

'Looks clean,' was his verdict.

'That surely is a relief,' Lucy said. 'You're sure?'

'As I can be. But I'm no doc.'

'Will you two stop fussing!'

Art Brown's tone had an uncustomary edge to it.

Seth Benteen had a dilemma. He needed to question his old friend closer. But not in the presence of Lucy. If Art Brown was the shooter, and he found it incredible to believe that he had been, he was also involved in the robbery of the gold, equally incredible to believe. And it followed, surely, that if he was tied in to the first two, he was almost certainly involved in Henry Blue's murder also. He did not want to have to march his old friend off to jail with Lucy standing by.

Fate intervened: Charles Barrington put in an appearance.

'Like to take breakfast with me, Lucy?' he asked.

'That would be very nice indeed, honey,' she responded, linking her arm through Barrington's.

'How's that leg of yours, Art?' Barrington enquired.

'Will everyone stop asking me about my leg!' Art Brown exploded.

Lucy quickly ushered her beau out of the store. 'See you soon, Uncle.'

Art Brown hobbled to the door to look after his niece and Barrington crossing the street to the café, scowling. He turned back to Benteen.

'Why the hell didn't you ask Lucy to marry you, Seth?' he growled. 'And I wouldn't have the problem I have now.'

'Problem, Art?'

'Yes. A nephew-in-law I don't want.'

'But he's a lawyer, Art. His poke will be a lot

fuller than a town marshal's. And I got the definite idea that you were ready to welcome him into the family.'

'Dollars can't buy happiness, Seth. And I don't reckon that Barrington is right for Lucy. Something about him that . . . Oh, I don't know,' he said frustratedly. 'Just can't put my finger on it, Seth. But it's there for sure.'

'Lucy looks pretty happy to me,' Benteen opined, seeing Lucy laugh at something Barrington said. Probably, he thought sourly, about the hick marshal.

'Shines on the outside, sure enough,' Brown said. 'But dying on the inside, I reckon.' He faced the marshal. 'Dying because you haven't asked her to be your wife.'

'You sure that it was only your leg you gashed last night, Art, and not your head? You heard her just now: she'd rather be in the company of a skunk.'

'That's her way of protecting herself from having to admit that she's in love with you, when it looks to her that you don't even know she exists.'

Art Brown's assertion, though welcome, only served to present the marshal with an even greater dilemma. If it was as the store-keeper said it was, marching her uncle to jail would surely reverse any feelings Lucy might have for him, pronto.

'Art,' Benteen began, heavy-shouldered, 'last night when I left your house, someone took a shot at me, and I'm lucky to be around.'

'Shot at you?' Brown's surprise seemed so genuine that he was either an ace actor, or truly stunned. 'Why? Who'd do that?'

'The why, I know. The who. . . ? Well, Pinkerton, that's the name of a mongrel who's taken to hanging round the jail, took off after this bushwhacker and got his teeth in him, you see. . . .'

'Well, it should be real easy to find the sidewinder so, Seth.'

'I figure, Art.'

After a moment of Benteen shifting from one leg to the other, the store-keeper observed, 'Are you dancing, or have you just got fleas in your pants, Seth?' Then, like a bolt out of the blue, Brown understood the reason for the marshal's unease. 'You think I'm the critter who tried to kill you, don't you?'

His question was couched in a mixture of disappointment and disbelief.

'Now why would I want to kill you, Seth?' he asked, disappointment now outweighing disbelief. 'I really did get this gash on my leg in the garden last night.'

'Art, I figure you should come along to the jail,' Benteen sighed. 'Until I get a handle on what's going on around here.'

'You're arresting me?'

'I guess I am, Art. And I'm real sorry.'

The store-keeper took off his apron. 'Don't be.

111

You're the marshal. You do what you think you have to do. No matter how darn stupid it is. What's the charge?'

'Attempted murder, for now,' the Jewel Creek lawman stated.

A man who had come into the store during the exchanges between Benteen and Brown now turned and hurried outside to announce to anyone in earshot.

'The marshal's arrested Art Brown for attempted murder.'

'Who'd he try to murder?' a passerby asked.

'The marshal!'

By the time Brown turned the key in the lock of the general store, the news had reached the cafe where Lucy was having breakfast. She caught up with Benteen halfway along the street.

'What's all this nonsense about my uncle trying to kill you?' she demanded to know of Benteen. 'Have you taken leave of your senses?'

Charles Barrington joined her.

'What evidence have you got?' he questioned. Seth Benteen told him. 'That's the flimsiest case I've ever heard,' he said. 'You won't be able to keep Art in jail on what amounts to your crazy ideas.'

Seth Benteen turned into the law office. Pinkerton came to meet him and growled on seeing Art Brown.

'Easy, dog,' Benteen said, in a calming voice.

112

'Do something, Charles!' Lucy demanded.

Pinkerton growled again, even more viciously.

'Looks like Pinkerton knows something about you, Art,' Benteen said remorsefully. 'You're welcome to visit any time, ma'am, once I get the paperwork done,' he told Lucy, before closing the door.

Pinkerton went and curled up under the desk. Benteen invited the store-keeper to sit in the chair opposite his at the desk.

'What now, Seth?' Brown asked.

'Now you tell me why you murdered Henry Blue, almost murdered me, and stole the gold. That's what's now, Art.'

Art Brown was aghast.

'Murdered Henry? What gold?'

'The gold that was in a cell back there,' Benteen pointed over his shoulder at the jail behind him. 'And I'll want the names of your cohorts, too.'

'Have you been supping, Seth?' Brown enquired, concerned.

'Supping! I ain't touched a drop of liquor since that day you gave me a job, Art. And that's God's honest truth.'

'Then there's only one other possible explanation. You've gone barking mad, Marshal! I didn't murder Henry Blue. I didn't try to murder you. And I'll be damned if I know what gold you're raving about.'

Seth Benteen rubbed the stubble on his chin.

The store-owner's denials had the ring of truth. Or was he hearing what he wanted to hear? Nothing would please him better than to open the door and let Art Brown walk out.

Brown studied Benteen closely.

'Seth, you're a man carrying a heavy burden. Want to share it with a friend?'

Benteen was at a crossroads. He had confided in Henry Blue, and now he was dead because of that confidence.

'Have you got a Bible?' Brown asked, when the marshal procrastinated.

'Right here in the desk drawer. Why?'

'Put it on the desk.'

Benteen did as Art Brown requested. Brown placed his hand on the Bible.

'Let me be damned for all eternity, if I'm lying,' he said. 'I swear by Almighty God, and on this Book, that I did none of the things you think I did, Seth.'

'Damn it, Art,' the Jewel Creek marshal groaned. 'I've got me a head that's spinning like a top.'

As Seth Benteen told Brown of the previous night's happenings, and the events that precipitated them, Art Brown's eyes grew wider by the second.

CHAPTER SEVENTEEN

'A woman you reckoned was Lucy?' Brown asked, when Benteen had finished, much to his embarrassment, his story about how he had been duped. 'Who turned out to be a man!'

'The devil who planned this whole thing, knew that I'd come running if I thought Lucy was in trouble, Art.'

Art Brown shook his head in wonder. 'This gent, whoever he was, must have been kind of dainty to pass himself off as a woman. Who do you figure stole the gold?'

'The Freedom Brotherhood, maybe,' the marshal said thoughtfully.

'The Freedom Brotherhood?' The store-keeper made no effort to hide his scepticism. 'That's all hooey, Seth. There's no such outfit.'

'I don't agree, Art,' Benteen proclaimed. 'The

stories about it have been going the rounds for too long not to have some substance.'

Brown began to pace the law-office.

'Well, if the Brotherhood exists, and they heisted the gold, that means that Jewel Creek has a Chapter.'

'A Chapter?'

'Yes, Seth. A Chapter is what the Brotherhood calls a branch.'

'Yeah?'

Seth Benteen could not help wonder, if the Brotherhood was all hooey, how Art Brown knew they had Chapters?

'Well, that's what the stories about the Brotherhood say these branches are called,' the store-keeper added, quickly. Had Art Brown realized his mistake and was trying to cover up his slip of the tongue? Brown went on: 'You know, Seth, if the Brotherhood does exist, that shipment of gold was probably to buy guns and explosives. Which means that this revolution they're supposed to be starting, can't be far off.'

Brown had just added another worry to Seth Benteen's fast growing mountain of worries.

'There have been stories about camps of men hiding out in the hills near the border, waiting to strike.'

'Seems to me that the hills near the Mex border as a starting point for this revolution would be kind of out of the way, Art.'

'There's logic to the choice of location if, as rumour has it, the Mexicans are allies of the Freedom Brotherhood.' Art Brown frowned. 'Maybe you should ask the governor for help, Seth. He could send troopers.'

Benteen shifted uneasily in his chair. He could do as Brown had suggested, but if the Brotherhood was a figment of over-active imaginations, he'd be the biggest fool in the West. And if he ignored the possibility that the gold shipment was for the Brotherhood and the revolution began, he'd still be the biggest fool in the West.

'Oh, don't fret, Seth,' Art Brown consoled the frowning marshal. 'The gold was probably heisted by everyday crooks.' He became thoughtful. 'Didn't Benny Creighton bust out of jail?'

Benteen had completely forgotten about the Creighton gang. But if it was the Creighton outfit who had robbed the gold, would it not be likely that Creighton would take the opportunity to settle the score between him and the gang-leader, and kill him as well as heisting the gold?

'That's surely a point to consider, Seth,' was Art Brown's opinion, when the marshal let his thoughts be known.

'I guess you best be moseying along home, Art,' Benteen said wearily. He grinned. 'By now Lucy's probably rounding up a party to come and bust you out of jail.'

'You look beat, Seth,' the store-keeper said as he

departed. 'I figure you should get some sleep before you fold up.'

'Sleep!' the Jewel Creek lawman exclaimed. 'My brain's going faster than a runaway train, Art.'

'Drop by the house for lunch,' Brown invited.

'If you don't let Lucy anyway near the cooking pot,' Benteen said. 'The temptation to poison me could prove too much for her to resist.'

'You're reading Lucy wrong, Seth. I reckon that she's pining for you. And all of her bluster is her way of hiding it.'

'You know, Art,' the marshal groaned. 'I figure you've got enough imagination to be one of them writer fellas.'

'See you for lunch at twelve-thirty sharp.'

He was at the door when Benteen said, 'A wagon left town after the robbery last night, Art.'

'How do you know that?'

'Tracks. The thieves were real smart *hombres.* Used a swish to wipe out the tracks, but I picked them up outside of town. I was on my way back here when I was bushwhacked.'

'Finding those tracks was real clever, Seth,' Brown complimented, quietly.

'It was Pinkerton here who gave me the idea,' the marshal said, patting the mongrel. 'I'd run into a dead end, when I saw Pinkerton's tail swishing the dust and it suddenly came to me that a swish might have been used to wipe out a wagon's tracks.'

The store-keeper chuckled. 'Maybe you should pin a deputy's badge on that mongrel, Seth.'

The Jewel Creek lawman laughed along with Art Brown.

'Smarter than most of my deputies, old Pinkerton,' he said.

Brown left. When he had gone, Seth Benteen sat quietly, feeling that the solution to the mayhem was right in front of him. Something he'd seen? Or something he'd thought about and had not recognized its importance when he had?

But what could it be?

CHAPTER EIGHTEEN

After lunch, Benteen made his way with Art and Lucy Brown to the cemetery to bury Henry Blue.

'Aren't you coming, Charles?' Lucy asked Barrington.

'Didn't really know the deceased,' had been his reply. 'And I've got a case to prepare for back in Hadley Wells, Lucy.'

It might have been fanciful thinking on his part, but Seth Benteen had the strangest notion that Charles Barrington remaining behind had not unduly perturbed Lucy. Lunch had been quite a pleasant affair, and Barrington's absence from the table, while he rode out of town on some errand, made the meal all the more enjoyable. Art Brown had made his excuses after lunch and left for his den, but not before he gave the marshal a broad wink. It suprised Seth that, on their own, Lucy became a most pleasant hostess.

Benteen reined in his soaring spirits. He was

thinking like a wet-behind-the-ears youngster. Lucy Brown had been pleasant to him because it was her duty to be. Her uncle would have expected nothing less.

The afternoon became suitably grey for a funeral, with brooding storm clouds rolling in to make a sombre occasion even more downcast. Most of the town turned out for Henry Blue's funeral. A lot of folk, particularly the poor in Jewel Creek, of which there were an increasing number, had lost a good friend in the town doctor who, in the tougher economic times that the town was experiencing, had had the doctor's services free of charge.

Looking the crowd over, Seth Benteen wondered if Henry's foul killer was among them. He saw Alice Walters weeping. It was Henry who had sat by her bed and nursed Alice through the terrible fever that had almost killed her and caused her hair to fall out. And it was Henry who, after seeing an advertisement in a newspaper which his sister had sent him from Boston, Henry's native place, had suggested to Alice that she should order a wig, and not remain locked inside the house all the time. Alongside her was her dapper husband Sidney Walters, a couple of inches shorter than Alice and more pretty with his smooth face and soft skin.

'Any more thoughts on who murdered Henry and stole that gold, Seth?' Art Brown enquired of the marshal as they made their way back down the hill to the town from the cemetery.

Benteen shook his head despondently.

'How about Pinkerton?' the store-keeper said in a tone that, to Seth's ears, sounded pretty close to mocking.

'Pinkerton?' Lucy asked.

'Seth's new deputy, Lucy.'

'I didn't know you had a new deputy, Seth,' Lucy said.

'He's not the two-legged variety,' Brown chuckled.

'He's talking about a mongrel I took in, Lucy,' the marshal explained, not appreciating her uncle's joshing one little bit.

'He's helping Seth to find Henry's killer,' Art Brown said, struggling to suppress his laughter. 'Among other things.'

At least the store-keeper had not blabbered about the heisting of the gold which, besides setting the town talking, would have made him look stupid in Lucy's eyes. And he also feared that were Lucy to become aware of the details of the previous night's fiasco at the jail, she'd not appreciate his mistaking one of the gang for her.

As he turned into the law-office, glad that he could be rid of Art Brown's company, Lucy said, 'We'll have leftovers for supper, Seth. If you care to drop by the house.'

Her invitation was issued just as Charles

Barrington put in an appearance. His displeasure at Lucy's gesture was plain. However, Seth Benteen couldn't care less. He was too busy sailing over the moon.

'That's mighty kind of you, Lucy,' Seth said. 'I'll look forward to it.'

Sidney and Alice Walters passed by.

'Howdy, Mr and Mrs Walters,' Lucy greeted them.

'Taking a stroll, Sidney?' Art Brown asked.

'Just a short one,' Alice Walters answered. 'Sidney has a headache. It's all the paperwork he has to do at the bank. Strains the eyes. Isn't that so, dear?'

Preoccupied with his own thoughts, Sidney Walters nodded absently.

'Enjoy your stroll,' Barrington said.

'T-t-thank you,' Sidney Walters replied with a nervous stutter. 'Come along, Alice,' he added, when his wife seemed set to continue the conversation.

'Don't be in such a hurry, dear,' Alice Walters gently rebuked her husband. 'It will only make your headache worse.' She turned her attention to Seth Benteen. 'Any ideas on who murdered poor Henry, Marshal?'

'I'm giving it a lot of thought, Mrs Walters. I'll catch the killer, of that you can be sure.'

'It's not easy to rest in bed at night with a killer on the loose,' Alice Walters said. 'I'm so lucky to

123

have Sidney to keep me safe. Aren't I, dear?'

'Such nice people,' Lucy Brown opined as she watched Sidney and Alice Walters stroll along the boardwalk.

'Come on, Lucy,' Art Brown said. 'We'd best open for business.'

'See you later, Seth,' Lucy said.

'Count on it, Lucy,' was his warm response.

As he went inside the law office, Seth Benteen stopped dead in his tracks, his whirling thoughts coming together in a rush. He hurried back outside. 'Lucy!' Puzzled by the marshal's strident summons, Lucy Brown spun around. 'Mind stepping inside the office for a moment?'

Her puzzlement deepening, she agreed.

'It's only Lucy I want to talk to, gents,' Benteen said, when Charles Barrington and Art Brown made to join her.

'What's all this about, Seth?' Lucy asked, the second she stepped into the marshal's office.

He quickly took her to the window.

'I want you to look carefully at Sidney Walters, Lucy. Tell me what your impressions are?'

'What in heaven's name has got into you, Seth?' she said, worriedly.

'Look, Lucy,' he said.

'I'm looking.'

'So what do you see?'

'Sidney and Alice Walters, Seth.'

'How would you describe Sidney Walters, Lucy?'

124

Lucy cocked her pert nose. 'Dapper. Dainty, for a man, I guess.'

'Put Sidney Walters in a dress and a blonde wig, Lucy. What do you see?' Lucy Brown looked at Seth Benteen, bewildered. 'In the dark, would he pass as a woman at a glance?'

'What in tarnation are you on about, Seth?'

'Would he, Lucy?' Benteen pressed.

'Yes,' she said positively. 'He could. But why would he want to? What's all this about?' Benteen averted his gaze. 'Seth, tell me what all this is about!' she demanded.

With no way out, Benteen was forced to tell Lucy about the robbery and the role which he now believed Sidney Walters, in a dress and wearing one of his wife's blonde wigs, had played in the heist. At first Lucy was astonished. But, regaining her composure, she faced Benteen squarely and his dread became a reality.

'You thought that Sidney Walters was me?' she asked, blue eyes popping.

'It was dark. I got just a glimpse, Lucy.'

'Well, even at a glance, Seth Benteen,' she fumed. 'It isn't any compliment to think that Sidney Walters and I look alike!'

He caught her up as she strode to the door.

'But, don't you understand, Lucy?' he pleaded. 'I was so anxious that you were being harmed, that my only thought was to help you.'

Lucy Brown's indignation slipped away.

'Is that so?' she said. 'And why would you want to help me so badly, Seth?'

At that moment, the Jewel Creek marshal would have preferred facing the territory's toughest honcho, rather than put into words what had been in his heart for two years.

'Because I love you, Lucy,' he mumbled.

'What did you just say?'

'I said—'

'Stop mumbling and speak clearly,' she commanded.

'I said because I love you,' he shouted. 'Is that loud enough for you?'

'It would sound better from the top of a hill,' she said cockily. 'But I guess it will have to do. And you took long enough to say it.'

'You're not mad?'

'Now why would I be mad, Seth?' she said softly. 'Hearing what I've been waiting to hear for most of those two years.'

'Why didn't you ever say anything?'

'It's not a woman's place to chase a man, is it? You wouldn't want to have anything to do with a brazen trollop, would you, Seth?'

Seth Benteen took Lucy Brown in his arms. 'I guess not, Lucy.'

'Well, aren't you going to kiss me, Seth?' she said after a moment.

Benteen swallowed hard.

'I ain't much of a kisser, Lucy,' he warned her.

126

And after the kiss, she said, 'No, you aren't.' Then she grinned happily. 'But they say that practice makes perfect, Seth. So in that case, you'll need a whole lot of practice.'

He swept her up in his arms. 'In that case, I reckon the sooner I start the better.'

His head to one side, Pinkerton looked on at the strange human ritual. Bored, he whimpered and rolled over.

'Now, you run along,' Benteen told Lucy at the end of yet another feverish clinch. 'I've got business to attend to.'

'You'll be careful, Seth, won't you?' Lucy fretted, sensing trouble coming.

'I have every reason to be. Now that I know where I stand with you, Lucy,' he said.

Alice opened the front door of the Walters' house, uninhibitedly surprised on seeing her caller. 'Marshal Benteen. To what do we owe your visit?' she enquired in her nervous way.

'Ma'am.' Benteen tipped the brim of his hat. 'I'd like to talk to Mr Walters.'

'Talk to Sidney?' Alice Walters was astonished that the law should want to talk to her husband. 'Might I ask why, Marshal?'

'It's OK, dear.' Sidney Walters appeared from a room at the end of the hall with a weary droop to his narrow shoulders. 'I think I know why the marshal has called.' He indicated the room from which he had come. 'If you would, Marshal Benteen.'

On entering the sitting-room, Sidney Walters quickly closed the room door.

'I know why you're here, Marshal,' he said. 'I've always thought you to be an intelligent man, and I knew that it would only be a matter of time before you figured out what happened last night. In fact, when Alice and I stopped to converse outside the law office a little while ago, I could see the wheels in your head beginning to turn.'

'You played the part of the woman last night?'

'Yes, Marshal,' Walters said, sadly. 'Not very flattering that I could, is it? The West was never my country. I should have remained back East. I know people laugh behind my back because of my dandyish ways.' He was suddenly angry. 'You're not a man out here unless you smell of horse and sweat. Well, I don't like horses, and I can't abide the stench of perspiration.'

He went to look out the open window. The stiffish breeze flapped the drapes round him. Seth Benteen patiently waited for Walters to tell him what he wanted to know about the other members of the raiding party, the motive for the robbery, and most importantly, Henry Blue's murder.

Sidney Walters turned to face the marshal.

'I take it that you've heard of the Freedom Brotherhood, Marshal?'

'I've heard tell of them, yes,' Benteen

confirmed. 'Are you telling me that it was the Brotherhood who robbed the gold, Walters?'

'Oh, yes. But taking back what's yours is not robbery surely?'

'The gold was in my custody, and that makes it robbery in my book,' Benteen stated sternly. 'And I'm pretty sure that gold smuggling is a crime, too.'

'But we needed the gold to buy guns, Marshal. You can't have a revolution without guns.'

'I'd never have figured you to be a member of the Freedom Brotherhood, Walters.'

'You know, I don't really subscribe to the Brotherhood's cause. But, you see, in the Brotherhood I was accepted.'

'Did you murder Henry Blue?'

'Pity Henry had to die. But you played a part in his demise, Marshal, by confiding in him. The Chapter Leader saw Henry go into your office as he's often done when sleep evaded him since his wife died, such a kind and loving woman was Martha Blue. When he left, the Chapter Leader instinctively followed Henry home. But when the Chapter Leader showed his hand, the good doctor was not prepared to listen to reason, and threatened to tell you about the existence of a Chapter of the Brotherhood right here in Jewel Creek – the Chapter which had been given the task of starting the revolution by the Brotherhood's Grand Council.

'Faced with possible failure, should word get out about our plans, the Chapter Leader was left with no choice but to silence Henry Blue, once he had extracted from him the information he sought, of course.'

'What's the killer's name, Walters?' Seth Benteen asked grimly.

'You were in his company just a short time ago, Marshal.'

Seth Benteen paled. He could only be talking about Art Brown. A gun blasted. Sidney Walters clutched at his back. A second shot through the open window pitched him forward. He tried to speak to the marshal, but he had neither the time or the breath to do so.

Alice Walters burst into the sitting-room. She looked accusingly at Benteen, before her wails of anguish went up on seeing her dead husband.

'He was shot through the window, ma'am,' he told her.

The marshal was caught between comforting Alice Walters and chasing after her husband's killer. However, his choice quickly vanished, because by the time he had calmed Alice Walters, the killer was long gone. But it did not matter. Seth Benteen knew where to find him.

CHAPTER NINETEEN

On seeing Art Brown sitting on a rocker outside the general store with his injured leg on a cushion, being pampered by Lucy, Seth Benteen thought he had seen men with gall before, but no one with it in the proportion that Art Brown had it. Sitting as calmly as you please, just after back-shooting a man a short time before.

'Seth,' Lucy greeted Benteen warmly, as he stepped on to the porch of the general store. But her smile faded on seeing the marshal's grim countenance. 'What's wrong, Seth?' she enquired anxiously.

'Art Brown,' he growled. 'I'm arresting you for the murder of Henry Blue, the murder just now of Sidney Walters, and the robbing of the gold in my jail. Stand up!'

Lucy went immediately to comfort her uncle.

'I've never heard such nonsense!' she berated Benteen, her blue eyes aflame with fury.

'Easy, Lucy,' the store-keeper urged his niece. 'I thought we'd cleared all of this up, Seth? Well, at least Henry Blue's murder. And I don't know a thing either about the robbing of your gold. And Sidney Walters, you say?'

'Don't act the damn innocent, Brown,' Benteen growled, and shook his head. 'Never in my wildest dreams could I have figured you for a killer. A double killer at that!'

'He's not!' Lucy spat. 'Uncle Art could not have murdered Sidney Walters. He's been right here all the time.'

'I wouldn't expect you to say anything else, Lucy,' the marshal said.

'That'll be Miss Brown, Marshal,' she flung back.

What a cruel twist of fate it was, Benteen thought. Twenty minutes ago he had been kissing Lucy Brown, and now she hated his guts.

'Charles,' she called out to the store. Charles Barrington appeared in the door. 'Tell the marshal that Uncle Art's been sitting on this chair for the last half-hour at least.'

'That's so, Marshal,' Barrington confirmed.

Benteen turned round on hearing Pinkerton's snarl. 'Git,' he commanded, but the mongrel would not budge. 'What's gotten into you, dog?' the lawman said, when Pinkerton's snarl became even more fierce.

Then Seth Benteen's mind went back to when

he had previously arrested Art Brown. When he had ushered the store-keeper into the law office, Pinkerton had snarled then, too. And he had assumed that Pinkerton was growling at the store-keeper, because he was the man he had bitten the night before. But Charles Barrington had been right behind Art Brown, and the marshal now realized that it was at him that Pinkerton was snarling, like he was now. Benteen turned his attention back to Barrington.

'Can you verify that Mr Barrington was here all the time, Lucy?' he asked.

'Of course I can.'

'Did you see him?'

'See him?'

'Yes,' the marshal pressed.

'Well, no. Charles was helping out by doing the accounts in the back room behind the store.'

'Art, did you see him in the last half-hour?'

Art Brown shook his head.

Barrington scoffed. 'Are you suggesting that I murdered Sidney Walters, Marshal?'

'I know you did,' the Jewel Creek lawman grated. 'Because I told Lucy and Art about Walters' murder before you put in an appearance. And if you were in the back room all the time, you couldn't have heard me tell Art and Lucy about Sidney Walters murder. So how the hell could you know that Walters was dead? Unless you were right there outside his sitting-room window, pulling the trigger!'

'Seth's right, Charles,' Lucy said, shocked. 'You couldn't have known.'

'I don't have to listen to this nonsense!' Barrington protested, and turned back into the store.

'Hold it right there, mister!' Benteen ordered. Barrington stood stock still, but did not turn round. 'I reckon that you are the man that Sidney Walters was about to name as the Jewel Creek Chapter Leader for the Freedom Brotherhood.'

'I'd remind you that I live in Hadley Wells, Marshal.'

'And Sidney Walters said that it was the Chapter Leader who murdered Henry Blue,' Benteen went on, unfazed.

'You murdered Henry,' Art Brown exploded. 'I'll kill you myself, Barrington!'

'Charles, Chapter Leader of the Freedom Brotherhood?' Lucy said, astonished by the revelation. 'I thought stories about the Brotherhood were just that – stories.'

'And I figure, too, that when you roll up your sleeves and trouser legs, Pinkerton's teeth marks will be on you.'

'Do as the marshal asks, Charles,' Lucy said, when Barrington was reluctant to concede the marshal's request.

Cornered and done for, Barrington became boastful.

'Benteen is right in all he says, Lucy. Henry Blue

and Sidney Walters were expendable. Every man is, including me.'

Lucy staggered. An intense fire burned in Barrington's eyes.

'All that matters, is that the revolution will succeed and America will revert back to the doctrines of the glorious South. Slavery should never have been abolished. And this *democracy*,' he ranted. 'Is it fair that the scum of the earth should have exactly the same rights as men like me?'

'You are the scum of the earth!' Lucy Brown said. 'What could I ever have seen in a man like you?'

'More than I saw in you,' Barrington flung back, cruelly. 'I had to have an excuse to visit Jewel Creek, and you were that excuse. You don't think for one moment that I could have fallen in love with a woman from a hick town.'

His eyes glowed with a fanatical madness.

'One day I plan on being the President of the new Republic.' He looked at Lucy scornfully. 'Now what kind of a wife would a nobody like you be for the President of the New Order.'

'That's enough of your crazy ranting, Barrington,' Seth Benteen growled. 'You're headed for a gallows. Not the presidency.'

Charles Barrington's gaze shifted to the sixgun he had placed on a roll of cloth just inside the door of the store, as a sensible precaution against the nasty turn of events which had ensued. He could reach for the gun now, and would probably kill the marshal before he tumbled to his trickery. But he would prefer to get closer to the Colt instead of lunge for it. That way, when he turned on Benteen, surprise would give him a telling edge. Another couple of feet, that's all he'd need.

He wiped his brow, feigning faintness, and staggered into the store. He palmed the pistol, readied himself, and swung round on Benteen, hammer cocked, the trigger a smidgen from full depression.

'For the revolution!' he cried out.

Pinkerton's snarl as he leapt at Barrington was vicious. Bared teeth sank into his gun-hand arm. Barrington howled out in pain. He fell backwards under Pinkerton's charge and crashed against the counter. Trying to throw the dog off, he stumbled over a crate of goods that had just been delivered to the store and fell forward. The cocked sixgun exploded into his gut. Pinkerton sat on top of the dying man, snarling.

'Easy, Pinkerton,' Benteen said. 'Your job is done.'

Lucy went to comfort Barrington, cradling his head in her arms. Being able to forgive was what made Lucy Brown a woman apart, Seth Benteen thought.

Charles Barrington grinned with the sad hopelessness of the dying. 'Isn't it funny, Lucy?' he murmured. 'When you need a doctor there's never one around.'

His eyes closed and Lucy laid his head gently on the floor. Pale and shaking, she sought the comfort of Seth Benteen's arms to shed her tears. The marshal held her close to him. Art Brown looked at Benteen, and shook his head sagely.

When Lucy stopped weeping, the Jewel Creek lawman said, 'Art, I'm putting this fine woman in your care until I return. But then I intend making her my wife, if she'll have me.'

Lucy Brown's eyes glowed with happiness.

'I'll have you, Seth Benteen,' she said softly. 'Every little bit of you.'

'Until your return?' the store-keeper questioned, worriedly.

Seth Benteen's face set in grim lines.

'I've got to find that gold, before it's used to buy guns, Art,' he said.

'Telegraph the governor's office. He'll send troopers.'

'No time,' was Benteen's gritty conclusion.

He turned and headed for the livery.

'The livery's closed,' Art Brown informed him. 'Ned Blake must be down with something, I guess.' Benteen paused midstride.

'Of course! Where else would a wagon come from but from the livery! And Ned Blake is its driver.'

'Come back safe, Seth,' Lucy Brown fretted.

'I've got the whole world to come back to,' he

said, kissing Lucy deeply before mounting up and riding out on a search that he reckoned would need a mountain of good fortune to bring it to a successful conclusion. He knew who he was looking for. But finding Ned Blake and his wagon in the hills would not be easy. Blake had a sizeable head start on him, but a wagon in the hills would be unwieldy and slow-moving. However, there was not much consolation to be found in that fact. Because his progress would be delayed by his poor knowledge of the country's geography, his two years having been mostly spent within the environs of Jewel Creek and its immediate hinterland. And picking up Ned Blake's trail would not be easy, and would take time – time which was not on his side. Another drawback was that he was not the West's best tracker.

As Seth Benteen rode out of Jewel Creek, hope was in short supply.

CHAPTER TWENTY

As the day wore on, Benteen became more anxious about his slow progress. He must have searched every inch of ground since he had left Jewel Creek, but could not see a sign of wagon tracks, and all the time, as he drew nearer to the hills, the ground became increasingly stony which would make it even more difficult to pick up sign. He had checked with a couple of cabin dwellers and small farmers along the way, but no one had seen a wagon.

'You're searching for a needle in a haystack,' one of the men he had enquired from had said. 'There's more trails in these hills than lines on a ninety-year old's face.'

'You could hide a whole army in them there hills, and never know they was there,' was another man's disheartening opinion.

Spirits plummeting, Seth Benteen drew rein in the shade of a stand of pine to slug from his water canteen. He swung round in his saddle on hearing a twig crack. Benteen drew his rifle from its saddle scabbard and put a load in its breech.

'Show yourself,' he snarled.

A man from Jewel Creek whom he knew as Harry Walsh emerged from thicker trees to Benteen's right. Walsh had been the manager of the mine that had closed down.

'I'm not trouble, Marshal,' he said.

'How can I be sure of that, Walsh?' Benteen replied, conscious of the secret nature of the Freedom Brotherhood.

'I can help you,' Walsh stated. 'And you surely need help, Marshal.'

'I ain't denying that,' Benteen said.

'I know where Ned Blake is headed.'

'To know that you'd have to be a member of the Freedom Brotherhood.'

'I was,' Walsh confirmed, 'up to last night. Then I got to thinking about what kind of post-revolutionary country we'd have built on the murder of men like Henry Blue.'

'You kept pretty quiet for a convert, Walsh,' Benteen growled.

'I had to be sure that my wife and two girls were safe first. They left on the noon train. Then I had another chore to do before joining up with you.'

'What kind of chore?'

'I had to make sure that Ned Blake's family were safe. Charles Barrington had the Blake house

140

staked out. The two men watching the house were under his orders to kill Blake's wife and children, if Blake did not deliver the gold to its destination. I shot them both.'

'I'd say, under the circumstances, you did the right thing, Walsh,' Benteen opined. 'How did you get involved with the Freedom Brotherhood in the first place?'

'When the mine closed, things seemed pretty hopeless, Marshal. And a man without hope is often a foolish man. I thought the Brotherhood would bring worthwhile change. But all it will bring is more chaos and strife to a country still bleeding from the Civil War.'

'You know where Blake's headed, you say?'

'Yes. I can take you there. With any luck, we'll cut him off before he reaches his destination. I know these hills. I scouted every inch of them for the mining company.'

'Lead the way, Walsh,' Benteen said. 'But you won't mind if I keep this rifle on you. Because you could still be a member of the Brotherhood, spinning me a yarn.'

'You'd be a foolish man not to, Marshal,' he said, setting off ahead of Benteen. 'But keep your eyes peeled. The Brotherhood could show itself anywhere from now on.'

The climb through the hills was arduous. The sun beat down mercilessly, and the air became thin and hard to find. Walsh, a man who had spent the

141

last couple of years mostly behind a desk at the mine in Jewel Creek, found the going hard. And the fact that he'd give Benteen ten years and twenty pounds in weight, did not help him.

'We'd better hole up,' the marshal said, when Walsh began to flag dangerously.

'Do that and the gold will have been traded for guns, Marshal.' He drew rein and took a pencil and some paper from his pocket and began to draw a map. Finished, he handed the map to Benteen. 'Does that make sense?' he asked. And when the Jewel Creek marshal frowned. 'That's as plain as I can make it. If I topple out of my saddle, don't waste time on me. Just keep heading into these damn hills.'

He urged his mount forward, up the next and even steeper incline, dogged in his determination to reach their destination. Seth Benteen sheathed the rifle he had been holding on Harry Walsh, now convinced of Walsh's conversion.

'Far more to go?' Benteen enquired an hour later, when even he was feeling the weight of the afternoon pressing down on him. By now Walsh's face was mottled with the strain.

'Not far now, Marshal. See that rockface with a bulge in its middle, like a pregnant woman?' Benteen saw. 'Well, beyond that lies a canyon, and it was to that canyon that Ned Blake was to deliver the gold and make the exchange with the gun smugglers.'

Seth Benteen drew alongside Harry Walsh.

'Then you've gone far enough, I reckon, Walsh,' he said. 'Turn tail and head back down. You've got a wife and family waiting for you.'

Harry Walsh studied Benteen before he spoke. 'That's mighty generous of you, Marshal Benteen. I'm not deserving of such. Aren't you afraid that I might be lying?'

'If you are, I'll curse you to hell before I go there myself,' the Jewel Creek lawman said. 'But I reckon that you're not lying, Walsh.'

'And so I'm not, Marshal.'

'Git! Where are you headed?'

'Utah. My brother's place. He's been trying to interest me in what he calls some mighty interesting hills in his neck of the woods, that I'll probably find ore in. Maybe even gold, he dreams. I wish you luck, Marshal.'

'I guess I'm going to need it.' The Jewel Creek marshal sighed heavily. 'Come on, horse,' he coaxed the mare. 'Best get this over with.'

Seth Benteen continued up the narrow track. His eyes scanned the terrain ahead, around, and behind him. It worried him that he had come so far, unchallenged. Harry Walsh had said that they had used trails that were off the beaten track, and that might explain their trouble free ascent. But now he was within spitting distance of where Walsh said the exchange of gold for guns was to take place, and still he rode on unchallenged.

143

Had he misjudged Harry Walsh? Had Walsh led him straight into a trap that would be sprung any second now? His doubts about Walsh had barely surfaced when two Mexicans appeared on the trail ahead.

CHAPTER TWENTY-ONE

'*Amigo!*' one of the riders, a man with a belly that sagged on his saddle horn, hailed him. 'You are lost, my friend? Or' – his smile vanished, and his mood became mean – 'you are an inquisitive gringo?' He turned to the rider with him. 'What say you, Pedro?'

'I say he is trouble, Manuel,' Pedro opined. 'I theenk we should rip him open and leave him for the buzzards to feast on.'

Manuel laughed. 'My *compadre* is a very mistrusting man. So why don't you convince me that we should not do as he says, *amigo.*'

'I'm not your *amigo*, you son of a whore.'

The fat Mexican stiffened, his face suffused with anger. Benteen's strategy, the only one that came to mind, was to rile the Mexicans to the point of disregard.

'And you're the offspring of a mangy coyote,' he insulted the second Mexican, quickly wiping the sly smirk from his face, which had come when he had insulted the fat one.

'Yankee bastard!' Pedro screamed.

His hand dived for his gun. Benteen threw himself from his horse, grabbing the rifle as he did so. The Mexican's bullet ripped a chunk from his saddle horn that spun off, catching the marshal in the right shoulder. Intense pain shot along his arm and numbed his fingers. The rifle clattered from his grasp into the boulders alongside the trail, not too far away, but still too distant. Because by the time he reached it, he'd be a dead man. He drew his sixgun, but the excitedly dancing mare forced him to roll away. A bullet bit the ground near his face. A second bullet caught the heel of his boot as he scrambled for cover. Another shot rang out, followed by an agonized yell. The fat Mexican was swaying in his saddle, trying to make sense of the hole that had been punched in his left side in line with his heart. He toppled headlong from the saddle and his skull split open on a boulder. The second Mexican, caught between danger from the mysterious shooter and the threat from Seth Benteen as he drew a bead on him, was in a dilemma that proved fatal. Benteen's bullet punched a hole between the Mexican's eyes.

Walsh came from rocks at the side of the trail.

'Those shots will be heard,' he said, urgently.

'Quickly. Follow me.'

Time being of the essence, the Jewel Creek marshal did not argue. He did exactly as Harry Walsh had ordered him to do. After a breakneck ride along a trail that crumbled into a ravine as they rode it, they came to a shack.

'Inside,' Walsh said, dismounting quickly.

Walsh scattered the horses. Again, Benteen followed unquestioningly. But once inside the shack, he voiced his doubts about the suitability of their hideout.

'Hell, Walsh,' he complained. 'A volley of shots will see this shack disintegrate!'

Harry Walsh was rolling back a mat. He lifted some loose boards to reveal a stairway that seemed to go right down to the core of the earth.

'This shack belonged to a man called Isaac Lawton,' Walsh said. 'Used to be a colleague of mine. What you're looking into was a shaft he built, believing that there was gold to be found in this rock.' He pointed into the black hole. 'Isaac built the shack to cover the shaft. Spent day and night down there. Never found any gold. One day he went crazy and ran right into the ravine, chasing a giant-sized nugget.'

He climbed down the stairs.

'Come on, we'll be safe in here until dark.'

Seth Benteen did not doubt that they would probably be safe from two-legged critters. But he wasn't at all sure that the same would apply to critters who slid on their bellies.

'You have no choice, Benteen,' Walsh stated bluntly. 'If you want to save your hide.'

Benteen knew that Walsh had stated the truth, but he had never been one to skulk. Shrewdly guessing his thoughts, Walsh said, 'A dead man can't stop the revolution, Marshal.'

Seth Benteen followed Walsh down the stairs. He slid the floorboards back in place, pitching them into almost total darkness, the only relief coming from the light through the narrow divisions in the floorboards. He worried about the quality of the air in the shaft. It smelled sweet and mossy. And he knew that foul air crept up on a man, until he became unable to fight its sleep-inducing properties.

It was not long before they heard men arriving outside the shack. Seconds later the door of the shack was thrown open, slamming against the wall and sending reverberations throughout the flimsy structure that brought it to within a hair's-breadth of collapsing in on itself.

'Search the back room,' a man ordered, his voice tight with anger.

Boots hurried across the floor, showering Benteen and Walsh with dust. Both men pinched their nostrils to avoid sneezing. Through a crack in a floorboard immediately above him, the marshal could see the man who had given the order to search the back room, and his shock was total. He was looking at his friend and former fighting colleague from the governor's office – Frank Clinton. The man he would have dispatched the gold to!

'Empty,' the searcher of the back room called out.

'Where the hell did they get to?' Clinton ranted, agitatedly pacing the floor and sending more dust into the shaft underneath. 'Horses can't fly. And they can't have vanished into thin air. They've got to be around here somewhere.'

Seth Benteen watched in alarm as Harry Walsh struggled to fight off a sneeze. Then there was a greater worry than Walsh sneezing. Benteen saw the glistening button eyes in the dark, followed by a rattle.

They had a rattlesnake for company.

'Did you hear something?' Clinton asked anyone who could answer his question.

'Rattler,' a man confirmed. 'There's probably a whole nest of them under this shack. We probably woke them up stomping around.'

'Well, this will really wake them up.'

On hearing a gun being cocked, Benteen and Walsh went rigid. Several bullets punctured the floorboards. Lead buzzed inside the shaft, but miraculously the two men were unharmed. The thunder in the shaft sent the rattler sliding for cover.

'Let's ride,' Clinton ordered, and the men filed

out of the cabin.

As the men rode away, two of the shattered floor-boards disintegrated, showering debris down on Benteen and Walsh. Had the boards shattered seconds before, they would have been revealed as helpless sitting targets.

'You know, Walsh,' Seth Benteen said, relieved, 'maybe Lady Luck is riding with us, my friend.'

Harry Walsh stiffened, his grin turning to a grimace. He grabbed his side, and sweat immediately broke on his forehead. The familiar rattle sounded. Benteen grabbed hold of Walsh and hauled him up into the cabin. He tore open Walsh's shirt and swiftly slit the flesh where the rattlesnake had left its mark and sucked out the blood, spitting it out as soon as he tasted the salty fluid. He repeated the exercise several times.

'It's no use, Marshal,' Walsh said, his eyes already losing their light. 'He sunk those fangs right to the bone.' And when Benteen tried again to suck the blood from the wound, Walsh stopped him. 'There's no time to waste, Seth. If that revolution gets started, a lot of people will die and this country will sink into the abyss of dictatorship. Go. Go now! You've done all you can. I'll either be here when you get back. Or I'll be playing a harp.'

'Why did you come back, Harry?'

Benteen asked the question he had been wanting to ask since Harry Walsh had saved his hide.

'I had some crazy notion about righting the

wrong I've done, Seth,' he said, his voice weary and sad.

'Well, you've surely done that,' Seth Benteen said.

Harry Walsh lay back on the filthy floor, his breathing laboured. 'Tell Mary and the kids that I put things right, won't you?'

'You tell them yourself,' Benteen said. 'Because,' he picked Walsh up and carried him to the bed in the back room, 'I'm coming back for you, partner. I reckon I've sucked most of that rattler's poison out of you, so all you have to do is fight the little that's left.'

He paused in the room door to look back at the sad-eyed Walsh.

'Don't you dare die on me now!' he growled, and left.

Horseless, Benteen had to make his way on foot. But he soon learned that being without a horse was a blessing because, on foot, he was more flexible to suddenly changing circumstances, and it was easier to travel unnoticed through the hills crawling with men. It was almost dark when he reached the canyon. He crouched down in scrub, still without a plan as to what he could do to prevent the trade-off of gold for guns. And, of course, he could already be too late. Edging closer to the narrow entrance to the canyon, he saw a sentry perched on a ridge overlooking the entrance to the canyon.

He could see no way past the look-out. While pondering on his dilemma, a group of riders arrived who cut their horses loose into a corral and then made their way on into the canyon on foot. Once they had gone past his hiding place, Benteen brazenly attached himself to the men, hanging back a dozen paces, his hat low over his brow. It was a hell of a risk that could explode in his face at any second. As he neared the entrance to the canyon, he quickened his pace to give the sentry the impression that he was eager to catch up with the main body of men. He gave a friendly wave to the look-out, who waved back. It was dusk, and there was little risk of the sentry recognizing him as a stranger. And, of course, with the revolution about to start, the hills were full of men united by a cause, but strangers to each other. However, should one of the men just ahead as he closed the gap, turn, his charade would be revealed and he'd be full of lead in seconds.

The fact that he might be only seconds away from death made Seth Benteen shiver. Not so long ago, death would not have unduly troubled him. But now with Lucy Brown to go back to, the possibility troubled him greatly.

Immediately inside the entrance to the canyon, there was a chuck wagon. Continuing with his daring game, he collected a tin plate and took a helping of beans, rough brown bread and black coffee. It was food he could well do with, because his innards were touching. Grub in hand, he strolled to a boulder and sat against it. The mood in the camp was upbeat, and the talk was of the great victory to come. Careless talk told him that the revolt was set to begin at sun-up the next morning. The exchange of gold for guns had already taken place. The twenty wagons further along from where he was sitting were full of rifles and explosives. He spotted several Mexican army officers, sitting at a long table outside a huge tent, in discussion with the leaders of the revolt. The table held an array of maps, and the discussion was intense. He got up and rambled on, getting as near as he could to the parked wagons. As he progressed, he heard talk about the two Mexicans who had been shot earlier. But in the main, no one was giving the incident and the Mexican killers much thought.

'Who the hell cares,' one man said to Benteen. 'Anyone riding in here would be riding into firepower like no man's ever seen before.'

'You got that right, friend,' the marshal agreed in a friendly manner and passed on, getting nearer to the wagons all the time. But what the hell would he be able to do when he reached them?

Suddenly he was grabbed and hauled behind a tree.

'Holy shit!' Ned Blake growled, a knife against Benteen's windpipe. 'Never figured you were in the Brotherhood, Marshal.'

How should he play the hand now dealt him, Benteen wondered. Blake was angry. Should he pretend that he was a committed member of the Brotherhood? Or come clean with Blake and seek his help? Luckily for him, he did not have to make a decision.

'You bastards would have my wife and kids murdered. Well, when this revolution starts, there'll be one less soldier.'

Benteen felt the nick of the blade on his wind-pipe, as Ned Blake readied himself to shove it in. 'Your wife and the kids are safe, Ned.'

'You expect me to believe you?' Blake snorted.

'Just hold that knife steady for a moment longer, and I think I'll be able to convince you that I have nothing to do with the Freedom Brotherhood.'

'Yeah,' Blake said, suspiciously.

Seth Benteen told him about the happenings back in Jewel Creek, and Blake began to relax. 'What're you doing here?' he asked.

'Trying to stop a revolution,' the Jewel Creek lawman answered.

'That's the most loco thing I ever heard,' Blake said.

'Will you help me, Ned?'

Ned Blake did not have to think for long. 'I'll help you, Marshal. Any outfit that would kill women and kids ain't worth. . . .' He spat on the ground.

'Any ideas about how we go about this?' Benteen enquired.

'Come on.'

Ned Blake took him on a circuitous route to where the wagons were.

'The wagon with the red X on its side. That's chock full of explosives. If that goes up, most of this darn canyon will go with it.' He sighed. 'The thing is, how do we get it to explode?'

'I've got a way,' Benteen said, looking to where the Mexican officers and the leaders of the revolution were talking, not far away from where they were. Alongside them was a huge, blazing fire.

Catching the drift of his thoughts, Blake paled.

'The second you'd hit that fire, you'd be blown sky high, Marshal.'

'It's the only way,' Benteen said, grim-faced. 'And I'll not ask you to take part, Ned. You've got a wife and kids to go back to.'

Immediately, Seth Benteen ran for the wagon and climbed on board. He slapped the reins without mercy and the team surged forward. He turned the wagon towards the blazing fire. The group outside the tent were the first to realize what the sudden commotion meant, and began firing as he charged towards them. He was not an easy target on board the bucking wagon, as it swerved and twisted on the rocky canyon floor. As he closed on them the Mexican officers fled, quickly followed by the revolutionary leaders. Now gunfire

155

was opening up on all sides as Benteen's intention became obvious to all. As he drew near to the leaping flames of the fire, he swerved the wagon and leaped clear. Hitting the ground running, he opened up as much ground as he could between him and the wagon as it turned over on to the flames. A mighty explosion shook the ground, and brought half of the canyon tumbling down in a killer rush of rocks and boulders and flying shale as deadly as any bullet. Flaming debris showered over the other wagons, and the ammunition in them in turn exploded. Seth Benteen was carried away on waves of hot air and crashed to the ground, shaken, but in the main unharmed. Other men were not so lucky and lay limbless and dead. Some horribly burned.

Ned Blake charged through the raging flames, a saddled horse in tow.

'Get on board, Benteen,' he shouted.

Aching in every bone and joint, the Jewel Creek marshal made one final effort and vaulted into the saddle. Together they rode helter-skelter out of the canyon.

'Was that all the weapons, Blake?' Benteen asked, once free of the carnage.

'Yeah,' came his reassuring reply. 'Of course there's camps spread throughout the hills, but I reckon that now, with the guns gone, they'll disperse.'

Satisfied with his night's work, Seth Benteen

made tracks for the shack where he had left Harry Walsh. But he need not have bothered.

'We can't afford to hang around forever,' Blake reminded Benteen, when he lingered. 'The revolution might be over. But that won't stop them skinning us alive if they catch us up.'

Benteen buried Harry Walsh as best he could with rocks.

'Thanks, friend,' he said. 'Without you I couldn't have done this.'

Riding into Jewel Creek the next morning, Seth Benteen's attention was got by the eerie silence; a silence that was explained a few moments later when Benny Creighton stepped from the saloon, holding Lucy Brown hostage. Augie Sullivan and another snake-eyed honcho flanked Creighton on either side.

'I've come to settle with you, Benteen,' Creighton growled. 'First I'm going to kill the woman, then you.'

'Your fight is with me, Creighton,' the Jewel Creek marshal said. 'Let the woman go.'

Benny Creighton's laughter was ugly.

'Tell you what, lawman,' he said. 'I'll let the boys have their fun with her. After they're done, I reckon she'll beg me to kill her.'

'Did you harm her uncle?'

'Busted his head, but he'll be OK. His punishment is to live after this is over.'

Suddenly windows and doors along the street were opening, and from each window and door guns were poking. Wild-eyed, Creighton looked around. However, his sidekicks were even more wild-eyed at the unexpected turn of events.

'We ain't got no argument with you folks,' Augie Sullivan yelled, quickly heading for his horse, followed in spit-quick time by Snake-eye. Creighton shot them both in the back. Lucy took advantage of the confusion to break free of Creighton's clutches.

'That leaves just you and me, Creighton,' Marshal Seth Benteen said.

The Jewel Creek marshal's gun flashed from leather and exploded. Creighton was lifted off his feet and pitched into the street, his lifeless eyes stilled in surprise. Lucy ran to Seth's arms, and he held her close to him. Pinkerton charged from the law-office to join them. Folk crowded in to the street; good folk. Seth Benteen reckoned that Jewel Creek would be just fine.

Just fine, indeed.